A CHRISTMAS SHADOW

A CHIEF INSPECTOR SHADOW MYSTERY

H L Marsay

TULE
PUBLISHING

DEDICATION

For Charlie,
With love x

CHAPTER ONE

Across 3 (7 letters)
Mr E's Tin was used to make this cathedral

DETECTIVE CHIEF INSPECTOR John Shadow softly stamped his feet on the smooth stone floor, but it was no good. He could no longer feel his toes, and when he exhaled, his breath formed little clouds in front of his face. As he glanced over his shoulder, people dressed in coats, hats and scarves were still streaming in through the Minster's huge west doors. He couldn't recall ever seeing so many people crammed into the cavernous cathedral. The nave was full, and every chair was taken, so people spilled into the north and south transepts, perching on the stone benches carved into the alcoves. Yet, despite the crowds, it was still as cold inside the Minster as it was outside in the frosty, early December evening. Standing on his right-hand side was Maggie, his old schoolfriend. She was rubbing her hands together as the tip of her nose turned pink.

"I wish I'd worn some gloves," she whispered. "I'd forgotten how cold this place can be."

Shadow grunted in response. He had remembered very

well that the huge and ancient cathedral was chilly even on the hottest summer's day, but against his better judgement he had still let himself be talked into coming tonight. To his left were the couple responsible for his current frozen state. Jimmy and Sophie were wearing matching novelty jumpers featuring a pair of grinning reindeer and seemed oblivious to the Arctic-like temperature. They were due to be married in the Minster on Saturday and had asked Shadow and Maggie to join them at tonight's Advent Procession. Angela, Jimmy's sister, and Tom, one of the constables from the station, were present too, sitting on Maggie's other side.

A new dean had recently arrived at the Minster. She would be conducting the wedding service and had personally invited Sophie and Jimmy to join her after the Minster's famous procession for mince pies and mulled wine in the Chapter House. As neither Jimmy's mother nor Sophie's parents could attend, they had asked their friends to come along instead.

"Do you think they'll sing 'Away in a Manger'?" asked Jimmy as he studied the neatly printed order of service.

Shadow shook his head. As so often happened, his sergeant's enthusiasm had led him down the wrong path. "No, it's not a carol service." He tutted. "Traditionally the church doesn't sing carols until Christmas Eve."

"That's a shame," replied Jimmy, but before he could say more, he suddenly sprang to his feet and began waving at two figures, one short and one tall, pushing their way through the crowded nave towards them.

"What are they doing here?" groaned Shadow. Despite being half hidden by their woolly hats and brightly coloured scarves wrapped around their faces, it was impossible not to recognise the two forensic scientists they worked with, Ben and Ollie, or as Shadow privately called them, Laurel and Hardy.

"We invited them too. They're both going to be my best men, Chief, and James and Henry, Sophie's brothers, are going to be my ushers, but they couldn't make it. I said we'd save Ben and Ollie a seat," explained Jimmy as he began shuffling along to make room for his friends. Shadow raised his eyes heavenward to the vaulted roof high above his head.

"Best men! Talk about a contradiction in terms. You would have been better enlisting two police dogs if you want your guests to get to the correct seats and don't want the rings to go astray," he muttered as the two accident-prone scientists joined them. The eight of them were now crammed together into a single pew.

"How long do you think this thing will go on for?" Shadow whispered to Maggie as he frowned at his own order of service.

"Stop being so grumpy. People have come from all over the country to be here. You never know, you might enjoy it," she hissed back, "and remember we are here for moral support," she added, nodding towards Jimmy and Sophie.

Shadow was about to query how much moral support a

detective and a doctor really needed when suddenly the crowd fell silent as the new dean in her red and gold flowing robes appeared in the pulpit.

In a loud, clear voice she welcomed the congregation and made what she referred to as "housekeeping" announcements regarding the location of the fire exits and what to do at the end of the service. When she had finished, she stepped down and made her way to the vestry. As her footsteps echoed away, the lights inside the Minster were turned out one by one until the vast space was plunged into a hushed darkness.

"Isn't it exciting?" whispered Jimmy and Maggie in unison on either side of him.

Shadow didn't feel any excitement, only an uncomfortable sense of foreboding. Perhaps it was the dean's reference to the fire exits combined with the fact that every one of the several thousand people present was holding an unlit candle. He could vividly remember being a teenager and watching from his bedroom in fascination and horror as fire ripped through the Minster following a lightning strike. He shuddered, but at that moment, the distant voices of the choir began to sing out and the first flickering flame could be seen. The flame was passed from person to person, following the choir's journey from east to west through the Minster.

Shadow heard Maggie's sharp intake of breath as the young choristers, with their long white robes and candlelit song sheets, came into view. They continued steadily on their way, followed by the dean and other members of the chapter. The golden glow from the lit candles began to slowly spread through the huge cathedral. Eventually, the flame reached their row. Now it was Shadow's turn to hold his breath as Ben lit Ollie's candle, who lit Sophie's and so on until he used his own flame to light Maggie's candle. She smiled up at him.

"Even you have to admit this is pretty special," she whispered before turning to light Angela's candle. Shadow, although not religious, had to agree that there was something spiritual about watching as the tiny flickering points of light broke through the darkness, and listening to the words and music of the service that had barely changed for hundreds of years. He leaned back, listening to the gospel readings and trying not to be concerned about the wax running down his candle at an alarming rate, then slowly spreading across the paper disc protecting his hand. Next to him Jimmy was having a similar problem, as he tried to keep his expensive trainers from being splattered by the hot, dripping wax.

Then just as the dean was solemnly completing her blessing of the congregation, there was a slight commotion as Ben managed to set fire to his order of service. Shadow shook his head in despair as his two colleagues tried to discreetly stamp on the burning piece of paper while Maggie stifled a giggle.

When the electric lights were finally switched back on, Shadow slowly rose to his feet. Thanks to the cold and the hard wooden seat, he felt like all of his joints needed oiling. He and the others waited until most of the congregation had left, then made their way through the nave towards the Chapter House, depositing their used candles in the waiting receptacles. Jimmy, Tom, Ben and Ollie paused under the huge advent wreath that was suspended in its traditional place below the Central Tower.

"Wow, how big do you think it is?" asked Jimmy. Ben squinted up and raised his hands as if trying to measure it.

"Three metres, maybe more," he estimated.

"It's four metres wide," said Angela. "I brought my class over on Friday to see it being winched into position," she explained. Angela taught the class of children that contained the probationer choristers at the Minster School on the other side of Deansgate, only a few steps from the Minster itself. "And before you ask, each of the four candles is a metre high."

"Next year you should bring those four too," Shadow whispered to her as the younger men continued staring as they now tried to guess the weight of the massive wreath. Shadow and Angela left them to it as they turned and followed Sophie and Maggie. On their way, Sophie pointed through the open doors into the Quire, the inner sanctum of the Minster and where the archbishop's throne was located.

"That's where we'll be getting married," she whispered. "Six days and counting."

"Are you nervous?" asked Maggie.

Sophie shook her head and smiled. "No, just excited." She tapped quickly on her mobile phone. "I'm making notes for the photographer so he knows where to get the best shots. We really wanted a photo on the city walls with the Minster in the background but he said it will be growing dark by the end of the ceremony and the walls close at dusk." She glanced back indulgently at her prospective husband. "It looks like we'll have to make do with a photo beneath the advent wreath instead."

They entered the Chapter House along with those who had taken part in the procession and a few dozen other members of the congregation, who had been invited to stay behind afterwards. There was a large table laden with plates piled high with mince pies and steaming pots of mulled wine ready to be ladled into the waiting glasses. In front of the table, the dean was smiling patiently as she waited to greet her guests. Sophie took Maggie and Angela over to introduce them. Shadow hung back and took the opportunity to wander around the Chapter House. Despite living in York for most of his life, he rarely visited the city's most famous building.

The Chapter House was a magnificent octagonal space with a high vaulted ceiling and some of the Minster's finest carvings. From his position at the edge of the room, he also had a chance to observe the new dean. Clarissa Fortescue was a rising star in the Church of England and widely tipped to become a future bishop. He recalled reading the *Yorkshire Post*'s profile on her when her appointment had been announced. Ten years ago, she had given up a highly successful career in one of London's top accountancy firms to join the church. She was married but had no children. She was a tall, imposing woman even without her ceremonial robes. Her steel-coloured hair was cropped short. She wore large tortoiseshell-framed glasses and as her smile widened, Shadow noticed her front teeth were slightly protruding.

"Mulled wine, Chief?" asked Jimmy, who had appeared next to him and was carefully balancing four glasses in his hands. Shadow wrinkled his nose and shook his head.

"No thank you. Why anyone thought it was a good idea to ruin perfectly good red wine by warming it up and sticking spices and bits of orange in it, I will never know."

"I quite agree with you, Chief Inspector," said a deep, smooth voice behind them. The two detectives turned around to find a man with chiselled features and slicked-back dark hair standing there. He was wearing a polo-neck jumper under a corduroy jacket. Shadow guessed he was in his mid-fifties.

"Hello, Mr Fortescue," said Jimmy.

"Good to see you again, Jimmy," said the man, patting Jimmy on the back while extending his other hand to Shadow. "I'm Simon Fortescue. It's good to meet you, Chief Inspector. Jimmy said he'd be bringing you along tonight. Now why don't I rustle up a decent glass of red for us both." He leant forward and lowered his voice conspiratorially. "Truth be told, Clarissa isn't a fan of the glühwein either."

"Thank you, Mr Fortescue. That's very kind of you,"

replied Shadow.

"Excellent! I'll be back in a jiffy!" declared Fortescue before disappearing into the crowd.

"That's the dean's husband," whispered Jimmy as they watched Simon Fortescue make his way out of the Chapter House, shaking hands and smiling at people as he went.

"So I gathered," replied Shadow, frowning slightly. "I think I've seen him somewhere before though. He isn't from round here, is he?"

"No, I don't think so. He used to teach drama down in London, but Sophie said he was an actor when he was younger. Maybe you saw him in something. Will you excuse me a second, Chief? I want to take these drinks over to Sophie and Maggie before I drop them."

Jimmy hurried away. To avoid the possibility of anyone trying to start a conversation with him, Shadow turned and began studying the stone carvings of mythical beasts and medieval heads above the stalls that lined the walls. A few moments later, he glanced over his shoulder and noticed Simon Fortescue handing a glass of wine to his wife. Shadow sighed. It looked like he'd been forgotten. Just then he felt a tap on his shoulder. He turned and was surprised to see a familiar figure holding a glass of red wine.

"George! What are you doing here? And why are you in uniform?"

Sergeant George Hedley had been the longest serving officer at York police station until a car accident he was involved in during the summer had led to his retirement. He had worked in the station's records office for years and was one of the few people Shadow considered a friend.

"I joined the Minster Police about a month ago," George explained as he handed over a glass of red wine. "Here, Fortescue asked me to give you this."

"Thanks. What happened to taking it easy?" asked Shadow, accepting the glass gratefully.

"I was bored within a week," admitted George with a smile. "I did a bit of gardening, we went on a couple of holidays, but then Carol said I was starting to get under her feet, being at home all day, so I signed up here. I only do three days a week and cover for special events, but it's good to feel useful again."

Shadow nodded. The Minster was one of the few cathedrals in the world to have its own police force. Most of its members were retired former officers. He took a sip of his wine and managed to stop himself grimacing. He could almost feel it dissolving the enamel on his teeth. Not wanting to appear ungracious, he glanced around to see if there was somewhere to discreetly deposit his glass when suddenly there was a commotion on the other side of the room. There was a gasp and the sound of smashing glass, and Shadow turned in time to see the dean collapse to the floor clutching her throat. He and George rushed over, but Sophie was already kneeling by her side and Jimmy was calling an ambulance.

"What's wrong with her?" asked Shadow.

"We were just talking to her, she took a sip of wine, and a second later, she didn't seem able to breathe," explained Maggie.

"She's had some sort of reaction," said Sophie. At that moment, Simon Fortescue – carrying a bottle of wine – hurriedly pushed his way through the group of people surrounding his wife. He dropped to his knees, put down the bottle and began rummaging through his wife's handbag that she had dropped as she fell. He pulled out an EpiPen, then he swiftly and firmly jabbed it into his wife's thigh.

"She suffers from allergies," he explained, slightly breathless. "Clarissa! Clarissa! Open your eyes, darling," he said as he cradled the dean's head.

"What is she allergic to?" asked Sophie.

"Nuts mainly, peanuts," said Simon as he continued to stroke his wife's hair. They all waited and watched anxiously for a few seconds as Clarissa's breathing began to return to normal and her eyes flickered open. In the distance, the wail of an ambulance siren was getting closer.

"We need to make some space for the paramedics," said Sophie as she took the dean's pulse. George nodded and with the help of Jimmy and Tom began clearing the Chapter House of the curious onlookers. Maggie and Angela carefully started collecting the smashed pieces of the wine glass scattered across the floor while Simon and Sophie continued to attend to the dean. However, Shadow's attention was focused on the bottle of wine by Fortescue's feet.

"Is that the wine she was drinking?" he asked.

Simon Fortescue looked up. "Yes, I was on my way over to top up her glass," he said, sounding slightly distracted.

"And she wasn't eating anything?" Shadow asked as he bent down, pulled the sleeve of his coat down to cover his fingers and carefully picked up the bottle and studied the label.

"No, not a thing," replied Sophie.

At that moment, the paramedics arrived in the Chapter House. Shadow and the others stepped to one side to let them treat the dean. George returned accompanied by a tall, balding man wearing a cassock and a concerned expression.

"Oh, good heavens!" he exclaimed several times, wringing his hands before hurrying over to the now fully conscious dean and her husband.

"Who's that?" Shadow asked George quietly.

"Canon Hugh Marchman. He's been here for years. He's the canon treasurer," explained George. Shadow watched as the clergyman fussed over Clarissa and Simon Fortescue, and generally seemed to be getting in the way of the medics. Jimmy, Tom and Angela came over and joined him.

"Where are Ben and Ollie?" he asked. "I wanted to give them this bottle of wine so they can run some tests on it."

"They've left already, Chief. They're in the finals of a pub quiz tonight," explained Jimmy.

Shadow tutted and shook his head. "Typical! Just when I

needed them for once."

"I can put it in the office for safekeeping if you think it's worth them looking at it," offered George. Shadow handed the bottle over.

"Please, George, if you don't mind," he said.

"Do you think there's something dodgy about the wine, Chief?" asked Jimmy.

Shadow shrugged. "Well, something caused the dean to have an allergic reaction. Sophie said she wasn't eating anything, and I didn't think it tasted quite right when I took a sip."

"I'll let Ben and Ollie know what happened to the dean," offered Angela. "Tom and I are going to cheer them on."

"Thank you," said Shadow as she and Tom turned to leave.

"Wish them luck from us," Jimmy called after her.

"We may as well make a move too," said Shadow as Maggie and Sophie, who had been talking to the paramedics, joined them.

George took the fragments of broken glass from Maggie and led the four of them through a corridor. They passed an office where one of George's colleagues was monitoring the security cameras located around the Minster. Then he opened a door that led into the staff car park, behind the Chapter House, and wished them a good night. The four of them stepped out into the chilly night air as the full moon shone down from the inky black sky.

"Well, that wasn't quite how I expected the Advent Procession to end," Sophie said, taking Jimmy's arm as they crossed over on to College Street.

"It was certainly memorable," replied Shadow as they all watched the ambulance drive away down Goodramgate, this time without the flashing lights and sirens.

"Do you think she'll be all right?" asked Maggie.

Sophie nodded. "Yes, her pulse was fine. I spoke to the paramedics. They are taking her in for some tests and to keep her under observation for a few hours."

"Good," replied Maggie. "I thought she seemed very nice. Thank goodness her husband was there. He was quite the hero, acting so quickly."

"Speaking of acting," said Shadow, "didn't that used to be his job? I thought I recognised him. Was he in something famous?"

"Yes, he was in those commercials for that brand of Italian coffee about thirty years ago. They were really popular, like a mini soap opera. He played the charming English neighbour to the feisty Italian girl who had moved to London," explained Maggie.

Shadow nodded as he began to recall the adverts. He'd never been a big fan of television, but he remembered Luisa, his late girlfriend, had loved watching them.

Look, John, she'd tease, *it's like you and me.*

"I thought it was really impressive that Mr Fortescue knew exactly what to do too," said Jimmy, interrupting

Shadow's thoughts, "but what would have happened if he'd got it wrong? Could he have killed her?"

Sophie shook her head. "I don't think so. An accidental injection could impair blood flow and potentially cause tissue death, but it would likely only cause some numbness and tingling," explained Sophie.

Jimmy looked worried. "Maybe I should take an advanced first aid course or something. You know in case I ever need to inject you."

Shadow, who was notoriously squeamish, held up his hand. "Please, no more talk of injections or blood flowing. We're about to eat," he pleaded.

THEY CROSSED OVER on to Goodramgate and a few moments later Gino was showing them to their table in Catania, one of Shadow's favourite Italian restaurants. The promise of a meal there afterwards was the main reason he'd agreed to attend the Advent Procession in the first place. However, for once, he didn't immediately look at the specials board, but instead turned his attention to the wine list. He ran his finger down the names, until he found the one he was looking for.

"A bottle of the Greco Salice Salentino, please, Gino," he said.

"Excellent choice, my friend," replied Gino with a broad smile. Shadow and the others then gave him their food orders and he hurried away before returning with the wine.

Gino filled each of their glasses and Shadow raised his to his nose and sniffed before taking a tentative sip. Sophie picked up the bottle and began reading the label on the back.

"Greco Salice Salentino. An elegant blend of *negroamaro* and *malvasia nera*. From grapes grown by the Greco family on the hills of Salento. With a distinctive aroma of cocoa and leather, and warm black fruit notes on the palate. Sounds lovely. Where's Salento?" she asked.

"It's in the region of Puglia, where the cities of Brindisi and Lecce are," explained Shadow. "As you look at the map of Italy, it's the heel of the boot."

Sophie furrowed her brow.

"Greco Salice Salentino – I've heard the name before somewhere."

"Maybe you read it on the wine list here," suggested Jimmy. Sophie shook her head, then realisation dawned on her face.

"No, it was when I was talking to Donaldson. I bumped into him on Friday, after he'd finished a post-mortem. I asked him if it was anything interesting and, well, you know what he's like, he doesn't usually deign to discuss his work with me, but he was in a good mood because he was leaving for his villa in Portugal the next day." She paused and took a sip of her wine. "Anyway, he told me that he'd been working on a man who had died suddenly in a hotel room. He'd fallen and banged his head apparently. I asked if he was drunk or anything and Donaldson said he'd only had a glass or so and had knocked the rest over. It was this wine. I remember because Donaldson commented that it was a waste of a good bottle."

"As sympathetic as ever then." Jimmy laughed. "Why were you so keen to order this particular wine, Chief? It's really nice by the way."

"It was the one Simon Fortescue served to me and to the dean tonight. I thought when I tasted it, there was something wrong. It's a wine I know well." He paused. "It's made by Luisa's family," replied Shadow.

The table fell silent, and his three companions glanced at each other. Shadow never discussed his private life. They all knew about his Italian girlfriend who had died almost thirty years ago, but they had certainly never heard him mention her before. There was an uncomfortable pause. Shadow took another sip of wine, wishing he hadn't said anything.

Maggie was the first to speak. "Then perhaps you should contact them," she suggested gently.

"Whatever for?" replied Shadow gruffly.

"Because in this small city, at least one person we know of has died and another was taken ill straight after drinking their wine. Now that may be a coincidence, or it could mean there is a problem somewhere in the production process or the bottles have been tampered with. Either way, they should be told. People talk and these sorts of rumours can ruin a small business. And don't just take my word for it, Gino will tell you the same, won't you, Gino?" she said to the restaurant owner, who was busy clearing plates away from the table next to them.

"Yes, absolutely, one bad review or a report of someone becoming ill after visiting us can be very damaging. We have been stocking this wine for years but already I am thinking we should remove it after hearing about what happened to the dean tonight."

"Who supplies you? A wholesaler?" asked Shadow.

"No, we go direct to the producers, but a little while ago a young men offered a case to us at a very low price."

"Lower than the producers? How could they do that?"

"My thoughts exactly, which is why I did not buy from them," replied Gino as he carried the plates away.

Shadow turned to Sophie. "There was no reason to think the wine led to the death of the man Donaldson told you about, was there?"

"I don't think so. I can check his notes, but like Maggie said, it's a bit strange that the same sort of wine should be involved in two incidents in the space of a few days. Especially a wine that you can't simply pick up at the supermarket."

"And there are guys trying to sell it on the cheap," added Jimmy. "I think it might be worth contacting Luisa's family too, Chief."

Shadow didn't reply as he attacked his lasagne, but he knew his friends were right.

Chapter Two

Across 5 (4 letters)
Ned joins a priest under a bishop

THE NEXT MORNING, it was still dark when Shadow locked the door of *Florence*, the narrow boat he called home, and stepped on to the towpath. There was a dampness in the air and a low mist lay over the river. He pulled up the collar of his old wax jacket and thrust his hands deep into his pockets as he walked up the steps and crossed Skeldergate Bridge, heading as he did most mornings to Bettys tearooms.

An hour or so later, he'd finished his full English breakfast, but he was struggling with the morning's *Yorkshire Post* crossword. He couldn't concentrate. His head was occupied with the telephone call he knew he had to make but was dreading. Luisa Greco had shared his life for less than two years, before she was killed by a dangerous driver, but his time with her had been the happiest he'd known. Luisa's father had sent crates of the family wine over each month and the two of them rarely drank anything else. Since losing her, Shadow now only ever ordered a bottle on her birthday, and he hadn't heard from her family since they'd taken her body back to Italy. He had no idea how to begin a conversation with them after all these years. With a sigh of resignation, he put his pen away, folded the paper underneath his arm and made his way across St Helen's Square to the police station, where he found Jimmy hovering outside his office.

"Morning, Chief! Sophie has already been in touch. The man who died in the hotel was called David Smith. She said she'll let me know if she finds anything in Donaldson's notes about him, and I've found you the phone number for the Greco winery outside Lecce."

"I've already got the number," replied Shadow, producing a small, very battered address book from his coat pocket and laying it on the desk. Inside Luisa had scribbled her family's number down in her slightly chaotic writing. Jimmy picked it up and made a face as he began flicking through.

"This is ancient, Chief," he said. "Half the places you've got in here have closed down and the number you've got for the winery is wrong. Italy have updated their area codes. Besides the number on their website is a mobile. I've done some research online. Both Luisa's parents have passed away and the business is now run by her younger brother, Luca."

Shadow frowned. It was unsettling to hear Jimmy discussing Luisa's family so freely.

"Fine," he replied tersely, "I'll use the number you found then, but I'll call later. I want to go and speak to George again first."

And with that, he turned on his heel and headed back into St Helen's Square.

JIMMY WAS UNCHARACTERISTICALLY quiet as they made their way down Stonegate towards the Minster. If Shadow didn't know better, he'd say he was sulking. After the third deep sigh from his sergeant, Shadow couldn't stand it any longer.

"What's wrong with you? Pre-wedding nerves?" he asked.

Jimmy shook his head. "No, nothing like that, Chief. It's just that…well, I agree you should let the Grecos know what has happened here, but I'm not sure what we are investigating exactly," he replied with a shrug.

"Neither am I," said Shadow evenly, "but something doesn't seem quite right. The wine I drank in the Chapter House last night was definitely not Greco Salice Salentino. It tasted like paint stripper. So, either that particular bottle has been tampered with deliberately to target the dean or there's a batch of fake wine out there."

Jimmy sighed again.

"What?" asked Shadow, beginning to lose his patience.

"Well, fake Italian wine? It's not exactly the same as heroin or cocaine, is it?"

Now it was Shadow's turn to sigh. The previous month, Jimmy had spent a week on secondment in Leeds with

Inspector Grabowski of the National Crime Agency. Since he'd returned, he'd seemed dissatisfied and seemed to start every other sentence with the words "In Leeds".

"In Leeds," he began now as Shadow silently raised his eyes to the sky, "they'd be too busy with drugs and organised gangs to bother with this. Isn't it more of a trading standards problem anyway?"

"Possibly," agreed Shadow, not wanting to admit the connection to Luisa played a large part in why he was so interested in the wine. "But we don't have anything else to investigate at the moment. York is a small city, with low crime and low unemployment. Thankfully, compared to a lot of places we don't have much of a drugs problem. The Mafia or whoever simply aren't interested in us."

"It isn't only the Mafia. There are all sorts of criminal gangs operating over here. Albanians, other Eastern Europeans, even some from Asia and South America."

"Have you been watching those foreign crime dramas again?"

"No, but Sophie bought me a book about all the different types of criminal organisations that operate in the rest of Europe, so I've been reading up."

"Exactly. In the rest of Europe, on the Costa del Sol or inner-city London, not North Yorkshire. We should think ourselves lucky."

"Maybe so, but they are definitely operating in Leeds. Inspector Grabowski thinks there's an Albanian gang operating there, but they're clever. They hardly ever use mobiles or meet each other in public. We don't even know the leader's name. He's only young, but he's got white hair, so everyone calls him 'the snowman'."

Shadow snorted loudly. "The Snowman!" he scoffed. "A criminal is a criminal. Giving him a daft name only makes him sound more important and glamorous than he is. Have we learnt nothing since Jack the Ripper?"

Jimmy wasn't going to be put off.

"I think it's only a matter of time before these gangs try to infiltrate York, and we're not prepared. They'll see us as a soft target. In Leeds, there were surveillance teams, undercover teams and they have a network of informers to let them know if something dodgy is going on."

"We have informers," argued Shadow. He could never fault Jimmy's enthusiasm, but he was getting increasingly irritated by the direction this conversation was heading in. Jimmy shook his head again, not in the mood to be pacified.

"We have Bob, the window cleaner and a couple of guys who live on the streets. It's not the same, Chief."

"No, it's not," agreed Shadow. "Bob and co don't cost us anything, except the odd pork pie or a packet of cigarettes."

"Sometimes I think we should focus on the bigger picture. This wine business feels like we're clutching at straws," muttered Jimmy as they finally reached the Minster. They went through the car park to the rear entrance, where George buzzed them into the office used by the Minster Police. They found their old colleague sipping a mug of tea, alone except for a cat, who was sitting next to him and intently watching the images from the security cameras.

"Morning, George, have you still got the bottle of wine from last night?" asked Shadow.

"Yes, it's here waiting for you. I found the cork too and pushed it back in. I thought you might want the forensic lads to take a look at it. Oh, and I put all the glass Sophie and Maggie collected in that plastic box, in case they wanted to check that too."

"Excellent, thank you, George," said Shadow, patting his old friend on the back. "Have you heard how the dean is this morning?"

"Fine, but tired. She's spending a few hours resting at home this morning." George paused. "I think there's something else you should know. Someone has been sending her anonymous letters since she arrived."

"What sort of letters?" asked Jimmy, who was busy stroking the grumpy-looking cat.

"What we used to call poison pen letters," replied George. "They basically told her she wasn't welcome here. The first one arrived when she'd only been here a few days. There must have been about seven or eight in total."

"I don't suppose any of them mentioned poisoning her or referred to her allergies, did they?" asked Shadow hopefully.

George smiled and shook his head. "I'm afraid not, John.

No, they were vaguer. Lots of biblical references. 'Your days are numbered', 'Not welcome in God's house', 'Prepare for your appointment in Calvary', that sort of thing. The dean shrugged them off and threw them in the bin, but Mr Fortescue seemed worried. He said if any more came here, we should hand them straight to him."

Shadow looked puzzled as he glanced around the office. "Does the post for the dean and the Minster arrive here? I assumed it would go to the Deanery or the offices on Ogleforth."

"It does," agreed George, "but the poison pen letters didn't come through the post; they turned up in the collection boxes. There are about half a dozen locked wooden boxes situated around the Minster, for visitors or worshippers to put a donation in. It's the Minster Police's responsibility to empty them each day, so it was always one of us who found the letters. I suppose it's possible that they could have been left by a tourist, but I think it's more likely to be a regular worshipper, but that wouldn't narrow it down much – the daily services, particularly evensong, are always well attended."

Shadow nodded. "I see. Have any of these letters arrived recently?"

"Yes, I found one after the Advent Procession last night. What with all the excitement, I couldn't pass it on, so I locked it in the safe with all the money from the collection overnight, then I took it up to the Deanery after I accompanied Canon Hugh to the bank to deposit the money."

"Any idea what it said?"

"No, the envelope was sealed, but they all have the same fancy writing in black ink, so it was definitely from the same person. I handed it straight to Simon Fortescue. I gave him his mobile too. He'd left it the vestry, what with all the excitement last night. Unfortunately, it looked like someone had stood on it or something. The screen was all smashed."

Jimmy winced. "Poor guy! I'd be lost without my phone."

Shadow stood up to leave.

"By the way, who opened the bottle of wine?" he asked.

"Simon Fortescue. We've got a little kitchen here next to the office, where we can go and make a brew. He asked me to help him find a corkscrew and opened the bottle in there."

Shadow nodded as he picked up the wine and handed the box of broken glass to Jimmy.

"Right, we'll be going then. Thanks for your help, George."

"What do you think you're doing? You can't take that. It's Minster property," said a shrill voice behind them. Shadow and Jimmy turned to see a large woman, with long grey hair knotted into a bun on top of her head, standing in the doorway. Her hands were on her hips and her lips were tightly pursed.

"It's all right, Marjorie, they are the police," George explained patiently. "They are only taking away the wine and the glass the dean used last night. Chief Inspector Shadow and Sergeant Chang, this is Marjorie Prentis, administrator in the Minster's office. Marjorie was in charge of the catering arrangements last night."

Before George could say anything more, Marjorie interrupted him.

"The police! I thought you were the police! How many coppers does one cathedral need?" She turned and glared at Shadow and Jimmy. "I hope you two aren't here to point the finger at me! It wasn't my fault the poor dean collapsed like that. I baked the mince pies myself, and the mulled wine was made to my own recipe. There was none of that shop-bought rubbish. I'll have you know my kitchen is scrupulously clean and I know exactly what went into that mincemeat and there certainly weren't any nuts. As soon as the dean arrived, she let us know all about her allergies."

The woman's face had turned a deep shade of red as she barely paused for breath.

George held up his hands as if in surrender. "Marjorie, please calm down. Nobody is accusing you of anything."

"Good morning, Mrs Prentis," said Shadow politely, although the woman continued to survey the detectives suspiciously. "We believe there may be a problem with the red wine the dean was drinking last night, not the mince pies or the mulled wine. Would you be able to tell us who was responsible for purchasing the wine that was served after the Advent ceremony?"

"That would be Canon Hugh, our treasurer. He's responsible for all purchasing except for office supplies up to the value of twenty pounds; they are my responsibility. I hope you've signed a form to say you are taking those away, otherwise we won't be able to account for being a glass short next time I do an inventory." She turned her attention to Jimmy. "And don't you be upsetting the cat. He's very sensitive."

"I'm sorry, I was only stroking him," apologised Jimmy, taking a step back from the tabby. Shadow raised an eyebrow at George, who handed him a notepad and pen.

"Do you know where we could find Canon Marchman, Mrs Prentis?" asked Shadow as he scribbled his signature on the blank piece of paper.

Marjorie glanced at her watch. "He'll be at home. At ten o'clock he always pops back to have a cup of tea with Mrs Marchman and check she's all right. They live at number five Minster Court."

"Thank you very much. Goodbye, George," Shadow called over his shoulder as he edged past the slightly terrifying Marjorie Prentis, who showed no sign of moving from her position in the doorway. Jimmy followed him out into the car park, but they'd only taken a few steps when Shadow spotted Ben and Ollie heading towards them.

"What are you two doing here?" asked Shadow by way of a greeting.

"Morning, Chief. Morning, Jimmy," said Ben cheerfully.

"We got a message to meet you here. Something about a bottle of wine."

"Well, for once your timing is perfect. Here, take this," said Shadow, handing the bottle of wine over. "The dean is allergic to nuts and she had a reaction while she was drinking it last night. Find out if there's anything strange in the wine or the glass she was using. It smashed, but we have the pieces." He gestured to Jimmy, who handed the box to Ollie while Shadow continued, "Also, if you can, find out what grapes are used in that wine, I'm sure it's not what it says on the label."

"No problem, Chief. Wine tasting sounds right up our street," said Ollie.

Shadow scowled and began to walk away. Jimmy began to follow him, then stopped.

"By the way, how did quiz go last night? Did you win?" he asked.

"Come along," snapped Shadow before either of the scientists could reply, "we haven't got time for a chat. I want to speak to Canon Marchman and the dean."

He strode out of the car park and turned left on to Minster Yard, the hidden-away cobbled lane of Georgian buildings that housed various members of the clergy and other Minster officials.

"Who first, Chief?" asked Jimmy, trotting by his side past the black metal railings that ran alongside Dean's Park. Shadow was about to answer when a glossy black door to their right swung open and out stepped Canon Hugh Marchman, the treasurer.

"Goodbye, my darling, I'll be back in time for lunch," he called over his shoulder.

"Goodbye, Hugh dearest," responded a woman with a neat blonde bob, held back by a black velvet Alice band. She was in a wheelchair. The canon blew her a kiss before she closed the door behind him, then he turned and stopped in his tracks when he saw the two detectives standing there.

"Oh, hello there, gentlemen," he said, his smile fading.

"Good morning, Canon Marchman. I'm Chief Inspector Shadow and this is Sergeant Chang," said Shadow. "We were hoping to ask you a couple of questions, if you have moment?"

"Yes, yes, of course, I'm always happy to help," he said, but Shadow noticed he had started wringing his hands as he was doing last night.

"I understand you are responsible for purchasing the wine for the Minster, including the bottle the dean was drinking from when she was taken ill."

"The wine?" asked the canon, sounding surprised. "Oh yes, I buy the wine to be used in communion and for any functions the Minster holds."

"Do they come from the same supplier?"

"No, Chief Inspector. The communion wine comes for a specialist ecclesiastical supplier in London, but I try to support local business when it comes to the other wine. If I recall correctly the dean was drinking an Italian red last night?"

Shadow nodded and the canon continued.

"Then that bottle came from a case from a new supplier we have started using. I don't remember the name, but two young gentlemen recently opened a business on Lendal. They specialise in importing food and wine from Italy. Actually, one of them used to be a chorister here at the Minster. Their prices seemed reasonable and I saw it as an opportunity to assist a fledging enterprise." He adjusted his glasses and carried on. "They also seem thoroughly decent. I often see one of them handing out warm drinks to our homeless community."

"I see," replied Shadow, glancing across at Jimmy to check he was taking notes.

"I understand the dean has received some threatening letters since she took up her position."

"Yes," replied the canon. His face twitched as the hand wringing began again. "I heard about that. A very unpleasant business. I know Mr Fortescue was very concerned about them."

"But not the dean herself?"

"I can't really say, Chief Inspector. We never discussed it."

"May I also ask what you did after the dean was taken ill?"

"As soon as she left in the ambulance, I came straight

home, Chief Inspector. Gwyneth was here alone you see."

"Mrs Marchman didn't attend the Advent Procession with you?"

"No, she would have loved to, of course. She adores the music and seeing the young choristers, but the Minster is terribly draughty, and she does feel the cold so." He glanced back anxiously at the recently closed door.

"I see. Well, thank you for your time, Canon Marchman," said Shadow.

The canon gave a weak smile, before putting his head down and hurrying towards the Minster.

"Did the canon seem overly nervous to you?" asked Shadow as the two of them watched the clergyman disappear around the corner.

Jimmy shook his head. "No, I thought he seemed quite nice, and he obviously dotes on his wife. Some people get nervous being around the police. You know, sort of like white coat syndrome, when somebody's blood pressure goes up, just because they see a doctor coming towards them."

"Perhaps," pondered Shadow. "Let's go and see if the dean has anything else to say about these letters."

The Deanery was less than two minutes' walk from the Marchmans' house. It was a large, elegant double-gabled red-brick building. Largely hidden from public view, at the end of a long driveway, it was set in the middle of its own spacious garden within the park. Shadow was about to push open the large wrought-iron gate when he saw the front door open. Simon Fortescue stepped out and began walking rapidly towards them. He cut an elegant figure, wrapped up against the cold in a navy cashmere coat, red scarf and trilby. His head was down, and he seemed engrossed with what appeared to be a mobile phone in his hand. He hadn't noticed the two detectives standing at his gate. As he came closer, Shadow could see his handsome face was pale and drawn.

"Good morning, Mr Fortescue," he said loudly. Simon Fortescue looked up in surprise, then switched on an easy smile.

"Hello, Chief Inspector, Jimmy. What brings you two here?" he asked, opening the gate and stepping into the park.

"We were hoping to speak with the dean. How is she this morning?" asked Shadow.

"She's fine but resting at the moment before she has to attend a function later," replied Simon, gesturing to one of the upper windows of the Deanery with closed curtains. "We were at the hospital until eleven o'clock last night. I would really prefer it if you didn't disturb her."

"Of course," agreed Shadow. "We would have liked to speak to her about the threatening letters she's been receiving, but perhaps you can help us instead. I understand from George that he passed on the latest one this morning."

"Ah, yes, that's right. He's a good man, George," said Simon. Was it Shadow's imagination, or did he look almost relieved as he removed a white envelope from his coat pocket and handed it over. The envelope was addressed to Clarissa Fortescue, with no mention of her title. It was written in calligraphy and the black ink of the last e was slightly smudged. Shadow removed the letter and unfolded it. He read the contents written is the same elaborate script out loud.

"'A woman should learn in quietness and full submission. I do not permit a woman to teach or to have authority over a man; she must be silent. 1 Timothy 2:11–15.' A rather antiquated view," he said, refolding the letter.

"I'd say archaic," replied Simon. "The others were in a similar vein. Lots of Old Testament tosh. Real fire and brimstone stuff. Clarissa binned the first few and told the Minster Police to do the same with any other, but I said I wanted to see them in case they got more threatening."

"Any idea who sent them?" asked Jimmy.

Simon shrugged. "Some religious crackpot who doesn't like the idea of progress in the Church."

"Would you mind if I held on to this?" Shadow asked, slipping the letter back into the envelope.

"Yes, please do, Chief Inspector. But I'm afraid I really must be going. My phone got damaged somehow last night," he explained, showing them the badly cracked screen. "I need to take it to a repair shop and see if anything can be salvaged. It's how work contact me, you see. I'm a lecturer at the university."

"Of course, thank you for your time, Mr Fortescue," replied Shadow.

"Are you thinking what I'm thinking, Chief?" asked Jimmy as they watched Simon Fortescue stride away through Dean's Park.

"That a well-known writer of anonymous letters can be found not far from here, Sergeant?"

"Yep, and he was always a bit weird when it came to history and religion and stuff."

"Then let's go and pay Mr Webster a visit," said Shadow, turning on his heel and heading back towards the Minster.

MALCOLM WEBSTER WAS a tour guide, historian and author whose office in St William's College was opposite the Minster. He had been "a person of interest" during a murder investigation the previous October and had a history of sending threatening correspondence to prominent individuals.

"I can assure you, gentlemen, that since our last meeting I have not picked up a pen in anger," he insisted when the two detectives began to question him.

"Or tapped a keyboard?" queried Shadow.

"Ha ha," Webster barked out a laugh. "Very good, Chief Inspector. Now who is it I'm meant to have been in contact with?"

"Clarissa Fortescue, the new dean. Have you met her?"

asked Shadow, watching Webster's reaction closely. He certainly looked much better than when they had last interviewed him. His skin had a healthy glow, his eyes were no longer bloodshot and his office no longer stank of cigarette smoke and booze. Webster leaned back in his leather chair and raised an eyebrow at Shadow's news.

"No, I haven't had the pleasure," replied Webster. "Being a practising Roman Catholic, I rarely set foot in the Minster except for historical research. But oh dear me, threatening letters, that must have been rather an unpleasant welcome for the poor lady; however, as I said no such correspondence came from me. You are very welcome to perform any necessary checks though. Send in your forensic scientists, analyse my laptop for suspicious usage or check under my fingernails for any tell-tale signs of ink," offered the writer, clearly warming to his theme.

"That won't be necessary. Thank you for your time, Mr Webster," said Shadow wearily, rising to his feet. Without a formal complaint from the dean, he wasn't going to waste forensics' time, especially if Webster didn't worship in the Minster and he certainly seemed to have turned over a new leaf.

"Madam Dean doesn't seem to be having a very happy time in our fair city," continued Malcolm. "I hear she experienced a very nasty reaction to some wine last night. I do hope she is fully recovered?"

"Fortunately, Mr Fortescue was there. He got to her with

the EpiPen really quickly," explained Jimmy as he also stood up to leave.

"Did he really, Sergeant? Swooping in to administer assistance like Azrael, the winged angel."

Shadow had turned towards the door but stopped abruptly and looked back at Webster. "Isn't Azrael the angel of death?"

Webster smiled innocently. "Yes, Chief Inspector, in some cultures that is indeed how he is depicted."

Shadow frowned. "Is there something more you wanted to say, Mr Webster?" he asked.

Webster leaned back in his chair and, lacing his fingers, together rested them on his chest.

"Allow me to tell you a story, gentlemen."

Reluctantly, Shadow sank back into his chair with a sigh. Webster cleared his throat loudly.

"My tale takes place several months ago, as summer was slowly drawing to a close. I'm sure you recall the announcement of Mrs Fortescue's appointment had just been made."

Shadow nodded as he stifled a yawn. Meanwhile, Jimmy was leaning forward, a look of concentration etched on his face as he entered what Malcolm was saying into his electronic notebook.

"The weather then was unseasonably warm, almost an Indian summer. Harriet, my fiancée, and I decided to take advantage of this happy occurrence and take a trip to Harrogate."

"Oh wow!" interrupted Jimmy. "Are you and Professor Maxwell engaged? That's fantastic! Congratulations!"

Shadow tried to hide his impatience as a beaming Jimmy jumped to feet and shook Webster warmly by the hand. He was also a little surprised to hear that Harriet Maxwell, the chief constable's sister and head of the university's chemistry department, was taking on Webster. He supposed there was no accounting for taste. Shadow held out his hand half-heartedly too.

"Yes, congratulations, Mr Webster. Could you continue with your story, please?"

"Thank you, gentlemen, thank you. Your felicitations are most appreciated. Now where was I? Ah, yes, after an extremely pleasant stroll around the Royal Horticultural Society's Harlow Carr Gardens, we were lucky enough to secure a table for lunch, at the Drum and Monkey. Harriet is extremely partial to seafood, you understand, and to quote the good lady, 'their trout is to die for'. However, gentlemen, we were not the only ones enjoying a trip to Yorkshire's finest spa town. Ensconced at a table in the corner was Simon Fortescue and a young lady, who most definitely was not the dean."

"Could it have been his daughter or a niece maybe?" asked Jimmy, looking up with a frown.

Webster gave him a cynical smile. "I believe the Fortescues are childless, Sergeant, and well...how shall I put this? I know many uncles who have great affection for their nieces but would stop short of caressing their faces and spoon-feeding them honey parfait in public."

"Are you sure it was him?" asked Shadow.

"Absolutely, Chief Inspector. Harriet recognised him immediately. He had been for an interview at the university the previous day. He's a part-time lecturer in English and drama apparently. I understand when they lived in London, his wife's success in the city meant he could pursue his dream of acting for many years. Not that he could be described as the next Olivier. He appeared in several television commercials for a well-known brand of instant coffee I believe, and did the occasional bit of voice-over work, but then Mrs Fortescue found God and, well, it seems he doesn't pay as well as American accountancy firms. Hence the need for Mr Fortescue to look for more regular employment."

"Can you describe the woman he was with?" asked Shadow, not wanting to be drawn into gossiping with Webster, who was a frustrated thespian himself.

"Oh, if only I was in possession of the words to do her justice, Chief Inspector. Extremely beautiful. Tall, slim, a sheet of long blonde hair falling beyond her shoulders, cheekbones that could have been chiselled by Michelangelo himself and at least thirty years younger than her dining companion. Therefore, in conclusion, may I suggest that if there is someone who wishes the new dean ill, you should be looking a little closer to home, gentlemen."

"POOR MRS FORTESCUE," said Jimmy as the two detectives left Webster's office and headed back towards the Minster. "Just when I was thinking she and Simon were such a nice couple. Do you think she knows?"

"There may not be anything to know. We only have Webster's word that it was Simon Fortescue, and he doesn't exactly have a history of being a reliable source of information. Still, it's worth noting."

"I suppose so. Where to next, Chief?"

"Let's pay a visit to this place Canon Marchman bought the wine from. But first let's see what's happening over there," replied Shadow, pointing to where a small group of people were gathered in the pale winter sun by the south door of the Minster. Amongst them was the dean and Gwyneth Marchman. The two women turned and smiled as Shadow and Jimmy approached.

"Hello there, Jimmy, and you must be Chief Inspector Shadow. It's good to finally meet you," said the dean, walking towards them and holding out her hand. She looked perfectly healthy, if a little tired. Apart from two plasters on her fingers, Shadow assumed to cover cuts from the broken wine glass, and a slight limp in the leg her husband had jabbed the EpiPen into, there were no signs of the previous night's incident.

"May I also introduce you both to Gwyneth Marchman," she added, gesturing to the lady in the wheelchair next to her.

"How do you do," said the canon's wife in a soft voice. She was a thin, delicate-looking woman, who was half hidden beneath a thick tartan blanket. Both the detectives shook hands with her. Shadow thought she had a kind face, but she looked even more exhausted than Clarissa.

"How are you this morning? You gave us quite a fright last night," he said to the dean.

She gave an apologetic smile. "I'm sorry, Chief Inspector. I have lived with allergies all my life. I forget how distressing my reactions can be to those who aren't used to witnessing them. Fortunately, Simon is only too used to dealing with these incidents. I simply don't know what I'd do without him."

"We spoke to him earlier. He said you needed to rest after a late night in A and E."

The dean smiled indulgently.

"Oh, Simon has been an angel, but he does like to fuss over me. I was exhausted when we returned home last night, but Simon was still a little agitated. He was always the same before an opening night. I told him to take a sleeping pill and it seemed to do the trick. He slept like a log the second his head hit the pillow. Unfortunately, despite being so tired, I did have a rather unsettled night as is often the case when I've had a reaction. However, I'm quite recovered now, and besides I have a very important appointment. The statute of

Gerald the Minster cat is being unveiled and I've been asked to do the honours."

"Poor Gerald died last month. The place isn't the same without him," explained Gwyneth, sadly glancing towards several of the Minster stonemasons who were gathered around a plinth covered in a white sheet.

"If Gerald's dead, who was the cat I was stroking in the Minster Police room this morning?" asked Jimmy.

"That must have been Gerald's brother Donald, Sergeant. You are honoured if he let you touch him. He's very particular," said Gwyneth with a smile.

"May I ask why you were visiting the Minster Police? Has anything happened?" asked the dean, turning to Shadow.

"We wanted to ask a few questions about the wine you were drinking, in case it was contaminated in some way," he explained. "I was also concerned to hear you have been receiving anonymous threatening letters."

The dean began to shake her head. "Oh, you mustn't take those seriously. I'm certainly not going to. As for the wine, I'm sure if it was contaminated in any way, it was simply a case of human error," she replied.

"After all, to err is human," added Gwyneth.

"Perhaps," said Shadow evenly, "but as the wine came from a new supplier, we think it might be worth looking into. When I took a drink, I thought it tasted odd."

"He's a bit of an expert when it comes to Italian wine,"

chimed in Jimmy with a grin.

"Oh, are you an Italophile too, Chief Inspector?" asked Gwyneth eagerly.

"I suppose you could say that, Mrs Marchman," replied Shadow through gritted teeth. He would never understand his sergeant's need to share personal details with everyone he met.

"He certainly likes the food," added Jimmy, earning himself a scowl from Shadow. Gwyneth didn't seem to notice.

"I adore everything about Italy. We went there on our honeymoon. I joke to Hugh that I fell in love all over again. The art, the music, the architecture, the people, the way of life – everything. Have you ever visited the country, Chief Inspector?" she enquired.

"Sadly no," replied Shadow.

"I long to go there again," she said wistfully. "But this thing does make everything more difficult, not to mention expensive." She gestured towards her chair in frustration and Shadow wondered how long she had needed to use it. "Never mind, I'm sure we'll return one day and, in the meantime, I watch all documentaries and travel shows that I can find."

"Gwyneth my dear, what are you doing out here? You'll freeze!" called out Canon Marchman as he came hurrying out of the Minster towards them with another blanket in his hands.

"I'm fine, Hugh," insisted his wife as he began draping the blanket around her shoulders. "You know how I adored poor Gerald. I wouldn't miss the unveiling of his statue for the world. And how lucky are we to have been blessed with a dry day at this time of year."

"There's still a very chilly wind, my dear."

"Another husband who likes to fuss," whispered the dean to Shadow. "Ah, here comes the press. Finally, we can begin. Are the two of you joining us?" she asked. Shadow followed her gaze to where a photographer and a red-headed journalist were striding towards them across the Minster Plaza. The journalist was Kevin MacNab, the reporter for the *Herald*, York's local newspaper and one of Shadow's least favourite people.

"Thank you, but no, we should really continue our investigation," he said, backing away and giving the canon and his wife a wave goodbye. As they left the gathering outside the Minster behind, he turned his attention back to Jimmy.

"Right," he said. "What do we know about this place Canon Marchman bought the wine from?"

"I had a quick google while you were talking to the dean. It's called La Dolce Vita and it's the only place in the city that sells Greco Salice Salentino, except for some of the Italian restaurants. They've been open for about six months. The website looks pretty basic, but I've checked and they are advertising that particular wine as being available retail and wholesale."

"How much?"

"There isn't a price, and you can't order online. It says to contact them."

"Where is it?"

"Next to Lendal Cellars. They are practically our neighbours, Chief. I'm surprised you haven't been there. It sounds right up your street."

CHAPTER THREE

Across 2 (4 letters)
Wilma replaces Vera to produce something new from the vine

THE TWO DETECTIVES made their way slowly along Stonegate. The ancient street was thronged with Christmas shoppers. They arrived in St Helen's Square and negotiated their way past the huge Christmas tree and the equally large queue for Bettys.

Rather than enter the passageway that led to the old Guildhall where the police station was housed, they stepped beneath the black ornate iron arch that led down to Lendal Cellars, one of the city's most famous and popular pubs. The path leading down sloped steeply and was cobbled. It led them to a small courtyard and the door to Lendal Cellars. A little further along, there was a small flight of steps leading up to a shop painted in the red, white and green of the Italian flag with the name La Dolce Vita on a sign hanging above the door. Also, above the door was a small black and white plaque informing them that Tobias Barchester Wood-house was *licensed to sell beers, wines and spirits for consumption on or off the premises.*

As they were about to enter, an elderly man walking with a stick and wearing a black hat and long black coat stepped out. He held the door open for them. Shadow thanked him and wished him a good morning. The old man remained silent and simply raised his hat and nodded in response. When they stepped inside, Shadow was immediately struck by the sound of Dean Martin loudly singing "Baby It's Cold Outside".

"I told you it sounded like your kind of place. They're even playing your kind of music, Chief," whispered Jimmy with a grin. Shadow ignored him and instead took in his surroundings. The walls were painted a deep shade of red and the bright lights reflected harshly off the glass shelves holding jars and bottles of wine, pasta, olive oil and other Italian delicacies. There was a strong smell of coffee. In one corner was a small marble-topped bar with several 1950s-style chrome stools placed in front. Behind the bar were posters of Vespas and Lambrettas. There was also a gurgling coffee machine and an overweight young man with curly blond hair who was swaying to the music as he wiped down the counter. His garish waistcoat and red cravat clashed with his ruddy complexion. He looked up when he heard the door close and grinned.

"Hi, guys! Welcome to La Dolce Vita. Can I help you or are you happy to browse?"

Shadow removed his warrant card from his pocket and showed it to the young man.

"I'm Detective Chief Inspector Shadow and this is Detective Sergeant Chang. We'd like to speak with the owner, please."

The young man's smile vanished for a second. Then he quickly flicked the cloth he was using over his shoulder and held out his hand.

"Toby Woodhouse – I'm one of the owners. How can I help?"

"We'd like to ask you some questions about a certain brand of Italian wine you sell. Am I correct in thinking you supply Greco Salice Salentino to both your wholesale and retail customers?"

"Yes, that's right. It's not a crime is it though, guys? It's a cracking wine. Are either of you connoisseurs? Look, it's there on the shelf behind you," he said with a nervous laugh. Shadow glanced over his shoulder. About half a dozen bottles were neatly arranged on a shelf, which was covered in a thin layer of dust. Taped to the shelf was a handwritten note in black ink, describing the wine and the area it came from.

"One person, possibly two, have been taken ill after drinking from bottles we believe you supplied," he replied, picking up one of the bottles and examining it carefully.

"Who? I mean are you sure? Maybe they bought it somewhere else? We can't be the only shop to sell it. Did they have a receipt?" Toby was now speaking very quickly, and his face was growing redder as his eyes flicked from Shadow to Jimmy. Shadow ignored his questions.

"Clarissa Fortescue, the new dean at the Minster, had an allergic reaction after drinking some of the Salice Salentino you supplied. You do remember supplying Canon Marchman?"

"Um yes I think so," said Toby, scratching his head. "I think he took a case on approval, but it's really Joe who dealt with him."

Right on cue, another young man appeared from a door in the corner. He was tall and thin with a serious face and round steel-rimmed glasses. Dressed in jeans with his shirt sleeves rolled up, he was struggling under the weight of several heavy boxes that he gently placed on the floor.

"Is everything okay, Toby?" he asked, looking nervously at the two detectives.

"This is Joseph Ingham, my partner. Business partner that is – nothing else," Toby joked, but nobody else smiled. "Joe, this is Chief Inspector Shadow and Sergeant Chang. They said the dean had some sort of allergic reaction to the wine we supplied to the Minster."

"Oh, my goodness is she all right?" asked Joseph, wiping his hand across his sweaty brow and leaving it streaked with dirt.

"Yes, although she did require medical assistance," replied Jimmy, who had begun taking notes.

"Was it the sulphites?" asked Joe. "Most wines contain them. They act as a sort of preservative, but they can make a few people feel ill."

"We believe her reaction was due to a nut allergy," explained Shadow, glancing at the shelves that held jars of sugared almonds and bottles of peanut oil.

"Come on now, Chief Inspector." Toby awkwardly laughed. "Even if we stored the wine next to the nut products, which we don't, there's no way they could get through the foil and the cork." He turned to his colleague. "Is there?"

Joseph adjusted his glasses. "No, I don't think so."

"The other person we wanted to ask you about was a Mr David Smith. He was staying at one of the hotels in the city and was found with a bottle of Greco Salice Salentino. Do either of you remember selling it to him?"

"Was found with? What do you mean?" queried Joe.

"Unfortunately, Mr Smith died."

Joe looked as if he was about to reply, but Toby – his round face creased in concentration – spoke first.

"Do you mean the accountant? The guy who came to look at the books the other day?" he asked.

"Tell me about him," said Shadow, shooting Jimmy a warning look to remain silent. Neither of them knew what David Smith's occupation was, but Toby and Joe didn't need to be made aware of that.

"There's not much to tell. He was here for about an hour down in the office with Joe, on Thursday, I think it was," explained Toby, glancing at his partner to confirm this, but Joe's eyes were fixed on the floor. "He certainly didn't buy any wine from us. He wouldn't even have a coffee when I offered him one. If he had a bottle of Greco Salice Salentino with him when he died, he didn't get it from us."

Joseph gave a small cough. "Actually, Toby, he did. I gave it to him," he said. Looking a little sheepish, he turned to Shadow. "It was meant to be a thank you. You see Mr Smith had come to give me some advice and he wasn't charging me for the visit. I'm quite new to bookkeeping and I'd made a few mistakes. Nothing major, but he was very understanding about it and pointed me in the right direction."

"Had you met him before?" asked Shadow.

"No never, but as I said, I needed some professional advice. Someone recommended him – I forget who. He offered a free hour's consultation. I'm sorry to hear about his death. He seemed like a nice man. I can tell you he wasn't allergic to nuts though. He was sat right next to where we'd been decanting the peanut oil."

Shadow nodded.

"Can you tell us where you get the Greco Salice Salento from?" he asked.

"Direct from the producer over in Italy. Straight from the vineyard. No middleman," replied Toby promptly.

"Please may we see the receipt?" asked Shadow.

"Yes, of course. I'm sure I still have it somewhere. Shall I bring it round to the station when I find it?" offered Joe.

"We'll wait if you don't mind," insisted Shadow.

Joe and Toby glanced at each other.

"Okay," replied Joe. "Why don't you come down to the office and I'll try to find it for you."

Shadow and Jimmy followed Joe through the door he'd entered from and down a flight of steep stairs into the basement. It was large room that seemed to act as a kitchen and storeroom as well as an office.

"Sorry it's a bit of a mess down here. We usually have a cleaner who comes every weekday morning, but she's let us down today," he apologised.

Shadow looked around him. A bit of a mess was an understatement. The place was a complete tip. There were dirty plates and mugs piled up in the sink. A large Formica table was covered with corks, bottles and funnels of various sizes. Crates were stacked on top of each other on the floor and on a rickety-looking sofa. Shadow noted that one crate was stamped with the mark of the Greco vineyard. There were also at least a dozen bottles of cheap supermarket plonk lined up. In one corner there was a desk with a laptop balancing precariously on several files. Embedded into the wall above the desk was a safe. A single uncovered light bulb hung from the ceiling, casting a yellow glow over everything. There were no windows, but two doors opposite each other. One had a glass panel at the top so you could see out into the courtyard.

"Where does that lead to?" asked Shadow, pointing to the other door.

"It leads to an old tunnel, but we never use it," explained Joe as he started rummaging through one of the files. "It dates from the fifteenth century when goods would have arrived by river and were loaded from the boat through there. This place was originally a wine merchant's; that's what attracted us to it. You know, wanting to maintain the heritage. Ah, here it is," he said, extracting a sheet of paper from the file and handing it over to Shadow. The chief inspector scanned the neatly printed receipt for two cases of wine complete with the signature of Luca Greco, Luisa's brother, and what looked like a stain from a cup of coffee.

"I'm sorry, Chief Inspector. We don't have a photocopier," apologised Joe.

"I could take a photo with my phone?" offered Jimmy. Shadow nodded.

"Have you and Mr Woodhouse been in business together long?" he asked, wondering how on earth they managed to operate in such chaos.

"We got this place about eight months ago, but we couldn't open for a couple of months because I kept flunking the alcohol licence exam," said Toby, who had followed them down into the basement. "I've always been rubbish at exams. Joe's the brains of the operation. We were at school together here in York. We were both boarders at St John's, so we've known each other for years. We grew up together."

"What are all these empty bottles for?" asked Shadow, turning his attention to the large table that dominated the room.

"We buy olive oil, peanut oil and balsamic vinegar in

bulk, then decant them into these smaller, artisan-style bottles," explained Joe.

"So, was this where Mr Smith was sitting?" asked Jimmy, pointing to the two chairs that were tucked under the table.

"Yes, that's right. He was sitting next to those bottles of peanut oil for almost an hour. There's no way he had an allergy," Joe insisted.

"Do you keep records of who bought the Greco Salice Salentino?" asked Shadow, without much hope. He couldn't recall when he'd last visited such an unprofessional business.

Joe shook his head. "No, sorry, Chief Inspector," he apologised again.

"We've sold loads of the stuff. You can't expect us to re-member all our customers," said Toby, "I told you about Canon Marchman already," said Toby, "oh, and the hen-pecked husband bought a couple of bottles," he added with a laugh.

"Who's that?" asked Jimmy, looking puzzled.

"Neville Prentis. We call him the hen-pecked husband because he's terrified of his wife. Poor sod!" Toby chuckled.

"Prentis? Would that be the husband of Marjorie Pren-tis?" asked Shadow.

"That's the one! If you've met her, you'll know what I mean."

Shadow checked Jimmy was still noting all this down but didn't want to start gossiping about the Minster's fearsome administrator with these two young men. He decided to change tack.

"Is it true you were offering that particular wine to local Italian restaurants at a below the market price?"

"That was meant to be an introductory offer. A sweetener. Something to entice them to order from us in the future," said Toby. Shadow raised an eyebrow. The young man with his habit of over explaining everything was starting to irritate him.

"It was Toby's idea, but unfortunately, nobody took us up on it," explained Joe.

"Maybe I should have listened to Joe – he wasn't keen on the scheme. Like I said, he's the brains of the operation. If it was up to him, we'd be playing Vivaldi all day and have called this place something Latin."

"I studied the classics," said Joe, looking embarrassed. "Toby's more of a people person. He's better at dealing with customers."

Right on cue, the bell of the shop door rang, and Toby's bulky frame quickly disappeared back up the stairs as Joe went to replace the receipt in the file. Shadow felt a sharp poke in the ribs. He turned to see Jimmy pointing at a large box standing on the floor next to the door to the courtyard.

"Boric acid – it's used as a cutting agent for cocaine," Jimmy whispered. "They told me all about it when I was in Leeds."

Shadow tutted and shook his head. Not Leeds again!

"Now which one of us is clutching at straws?" he hissed

back.

At that moment, Joseph turned around and saw what they were looking at.

"That's a delivery we took in for Mr Patel, one of our neighbours," he explained. "Is there anything else I can help you with, gentlemen?"

"No, that's all for now, thank you, Mr Ingham," replied Shadow. "We are having the wine the dean drank analysed. We'll be in touch if we find anything untoward."

"Then I'll show you out," said Joe with a look of relief.

The young man led the two detectives back up the stairs and they nodded goodbye to Toby, who was busying serving a customer. As Shadow followed Jimmy out of the door, he almost bumped into a glamorous-looking woman with long black hair. She was wearing a full-length fur coat, bright red lipstick and an expression of utter fury on her face. Shadow apologised, stepped aside and held the door open for her, but she barely acknowledged him.

"Where is he?" she demanded as she stormed into the shop. "I told you to keep an eye on him, and you've let him wander off again."

"It's not my fault," protested Toby immediately. "He doesn't speak English and I don't speak Italian. How am I meant to stop him?"

Unfortunately, Shadow couldn't hear any more of the conversation as the door swung shut behind the angry woman, so a little reluctantly he followed Jimmy down the steps into the courtyard.

"What do you think, Chief?"

"That Messrs Ingham and Woodhouse are a pair of halfwits playing at being businessmen. I'll be amazed if this place is still operating in six months," replied Shadow tersely.

"At least we found out that Mr Smith got his bottle of wine from here," said Jimmy, who was already shivering and pulling on his gloves.

"But we still don't know if his death is at all suspicious and it would have been helpful to have the test results on that wine from our friends in forensics."

"Should we get back to the office and see if they or Sophie have anything to report?" asked his sergeant, obviously keen to return to the warmth of the station.

"Good idea. You do that, then we'll go and have a chat with Mr Prentis. Let's see if he has any of the wine he bought here. I'm going to get some lunch."

Jimmy hurried back up the cobbled path and Shadow ducked into Lendal Cellars. He ordered a steak and ale pie and a pint of Old Speckled Hen before taking a seat at one of the tables that lined the walls beneath the low vaulted brick ceilings. He sipped his pint and considered the morning's events and his visit to La Dolce Vita. The shop basement was a disgrace, and he was sure the food standards agency would have something to say about the way cooking oils were being decanted on that grubby table, but had Woodhouse and Ingham committed a crime? His first instinct was that they were trying to pass off cheap wine as something more expensive, but he had no solid proof.

According to the receipt he saw, they had received twenty-four bottles from Luisa's family. If Canon Marchman had taken twelve and there were six on the shop shelf and Mr Prentis taken a couple that meant there should only be four left over at the most, but Toby claimed they had sold loads. Was that simply bluster? The young man was certainly more talkative than his partner. He had also admitted quite happily that Joe was the more intelligent of the two. If that was the case, why hadn't Joe taken the licensing exams? That would have made more sense than missing out on two months' worth of sales.

Then there was Mr David Smith. If he was a local accountant, visiting Joe Ingham as a free initial consultation, why was he found in a hotel? Shadow took another sip of beer. It didn't make much sense and he still had no idea if this wine business had anything to do with the letters the dean had been receiving. All that was becoming clear was that it looked like he wouldn't be able to avoid contacting Luisa's family. At that moment, his food arrived, but before he could tuck in, Jimmy slid into the seat opposite him.

"News?" asked Shadow by way of a greeting. "Have Ben and Ollie come up with anything?

"No, not yet, Chief."

"I thought I was being optimistic," muttered Shadow as he broke the crust of the golden pastry with his fork.

"But Sophie called me. She wondered if we wanted to go and see Mr Smith when you've finished here?"

Shadow stared at his sergeant in horror, his fork halfway to his mouth.

"Seriously? Straight after lunch? I'll be ill."

"I said you'd probably say that," replied Jimmy with a grin.

"Has she found something?"

"She thinks so. She started reading Donaldson's notes. It seems Mr Smith was discovered in the bathroom of his suite at the Maison du Fleuve. He was wearing his robe and the floor was wet. It was assumed by the hotel staff who found him that he'd slipped and banged his head after having a shower and Donaldson concurred. The body is still in the morgue. It seems they are having difficulty tracing his next of kin. As nobody had claimed his body, Sophie thought she'd take a quick look. She didn't do a full examination, of course, but she did notice that the deceased still had ink on one of his index fingers. She thought that was weird if he'd just had a shower and there was no mention of it the original notes. Also, if he'd fallen, she would have expected there to be bruising to his back, as well as to his head, but there was nothing."

"Sounds like Donaldson could have messed up," said Shadow, not without pleasure. There was no love lost between himself and Sophie's pompous colleague. "Could Sophie tell if David Smith showed any signs of having any sort of allergic reaction?"

"She didn't think so and she checked the list of personal effects found at the hotel, there was no EpiPen or anything like that."

"Do we know anything else about him?"

Jimmy removed his electronic notebook from his pocket and began scrolling through.

"Mid to late fifties, average height and build, dark hair. He was a smoker and a drinker, but no underlying health conditions. There was alcohol in his blood but not an excessive amount."

Shadow held up his hand in protest. Jimmy grinned and reached over to help himself to one of the chips from Shadow's plate.

"You know, you could always order something yourself, Sergeant," growled Shadow.

"No, I shouldn't really, Chief. I'm supposed on a bit of a health kick before the wedding. You know, so I look my best," Jimmy replied, taking another chip. Shadow raised an eyebrow. His sergeant barely drank, didn't smoke and went running every morning. His only vices were an addiction to expensive trainers and takeaway coffees.

"Did Sophie say anything else?"

"Not really. She was a bit surprised when I said he was an accountant. She thought he would have done something a bit more glamorous."

"Why's that?"

"He used a sunbed, got regular manicures and he had a flash watch and wore quite a bit of gold jewellery. Not that any of that stops him being an accountant, but it was Sophie's first reaction."

Shadow nodded thoughtfully as he took his last mouthful.

"Why don't you speak to Tom? Ask him to look into this David Smith and check out his personal effects properly. Depending on what he finds, we can always ask the coroner to give Sophie permission to carry out another post-mortem."

"Donaldson won't like his work being questioned," said Jimmy as he began to dial Tom's number on his phone.

"No, he won't," agreed Shadow, his lips almost twitching into a smile.

ALTHOUGH IT WAS a cold day, it was at least dry, so Shadow insisted on walking the two and a half miles out to Rawcliffe, a suburb to the north of the city. Jimmy had discovered this was where Mr and Mrs Prentis lived. Shadow would have preferred to spend the time alone, working out what he was going to say when he phoned Luisa's family, but instead he had Jimmy trotting along next to him, wrapped up in hat, scarf and gloves and chatting away about his forthcoming nuptials.

"So, Chief, I've been thinking about my wedding speech. Any tips?"

"Keep it brief."

"Do you think I should open with a joke?"

"No, not unless it's a funny one."

"I'll work on a draft and run it by you."

"If you feel you must."

THE LAST OF the afternoon light was beginning to fade when a long hour later, they arrived at the Prentises' home. It was a red-brick semi-detached house, half hidden behind a privet hedge. Several garden gnomes were dotted along the edge of the short path that led to the front door. Jimmy took a moment to locate the door knocker behind the large Christmas wreath, before giving it a cheerful rat-a-tat-tat. A few seconds later, it was opened by a thin, nervous-looking man with a neat grey moustache.

"Mr Neville Prentis?" enquired Shadow. The man nodded his head. "I am Chief Inspector Shadow, and this is Sergeant Chang. We are here regarding some wine you bought recently." Shadow stopped suddenly as the man raised a finger to his lips, stepped outside and gently pulled the door closed behind him.

"Shush, come with me," he whispered, beckoning Jimmy and Shadow to follow him as he tiptoed around the house and through another small, wooden gate. The two detectives exchanged a confused glance but did as he said. Neville led them into the back garden. The curtains in the house were still open and as the bright lights shone out it was possible to make out a patio, lawn and neatly planted flower beds. In the corner of the garden was a white painted shed. Neville paused briefly and cast an anxious look back at the house before hurrying over to the shed and unlocking the door. He quickly ushered Shadow and Jimmy inside before locking the door after them.

The shed was much bigger inside than it appeared on the outside and as Shadow looked around, it gave him the feeling of being a refuge rather than simply a place of storage. Granted there were several gleaming forks, spades and hoes hooked on to nails on the back of the door and a watering can in the corner, but there was also a comfortable-looking armchair and net curtains hanging at the window. A large table held an old-fashioned record player, several small pots of paint and glue, and a row of neatly arranged paintbrushes. The back wall was covered in shelves holding model aeroplanes, which Shadow assumed Neville had built. More importantly, in the far corner there was also a wine rack holding at least a dozen bottles.

"Sorry, gentlemen, but I didn't want Marjorie, my wife, to hear us."

"Isn't she at work? We met her earlier at the Minster," explained Shadow.

"No, she only works mornings and helps out when the Minster has a special event. She's on the phone to her sister. Hopefully she won't notice I've gone."

"May I ask why you didn't want her to hear us?" enquired Shadow.

"Well, you said you wanted to talk about my wine," replied Neville, gesturing to the bottles behind him.

"Doesn't she know that you have bought the wine?" asked Jimmy before Shadow had a chance to reply. "Is she teetotal or something?"

Neville shuffled his feet and looked awkward. "No, not exactly. I mean she likes a sweet sherry on a Sunday and the odd glass of Baileys at Christmas, but the thing is Marjorie is in charge of the money, our accounts and bills, you see. It's always been that way, even when I was working, I never had a credit card or a chequebook. Marjorie takes care of everything and then gives me some spending money each week."

"Spending money?" queried Jimmy as he began taking notes.

"Yes, so I can treat myself," explained Neville as he opened the net curtains half an inch and peered out back towards the house.

"Treat yourself to model aeroplanes and wine?" suggested Shadow, who had been studying the mainly classical record collection and the labels on the wine. They were all Italian and certainly not your average cheap supermarket plonk. More importantly there were two bottles of the Greco Salice

Salentino.

"Exactly, my two great loves," agreed Neville, before looking embarrassed again, "but you see the thing is I have to give all the receipts to Marjorie and, well, she wouldn't approve if I spent too much on wine. I've always believed you get what you pay for, but she has very strict ideas on these things, and she doesn't think a bottle of wine should cost more than eight pounds."

Shadow raised an eyebrow. He knew for a fact that several bottles in the rack cost more than double that.

"So?" he prompted.

"Well, I used to have to wait until the supermarkets had the decent bottles on sale, but then I found a new place next to Lendal Cellars."

"La Dolce Vita?" asked Jimmy, earning himself a scowl from Shadow, who hated it when witnesses were interrupted.

"That's it," agreed Neville. "They had a lovely selection of wine and the two lads in there seemed nice, so I explained my predicament and they agreed to help me out with a little creative accounting."

"Creative how?" asked Shadow.

"I pay the asking price in cash and they write me a receipt for seven or eight pounds. They know I won't be bringing it back and Marjorie is none the wiser, so everyone is happy."

Shadow wasn't sure the tax man would be at all happy with this arrangement, but he refrained from saying so.

"It has meant I've had to forgo some of the modelling kits I would have liked, but I think it's worth it," continued Neville with a small smile as he glanced lovingly at the wine rack.

"Were all these bottles purchased from La Dolce Vita?" asked Shadow.

"Yes," replied Neville, "I'm building up quite a collection. I haven't opened any yet though. I'm going to wait until Christmas, a little present to myself. On Christmas Eve, while Marjorie is busy as the Minster, I shall be in here with a bottle or two, listening to my favourite recording of Handel's *Messiah*."

"Do you suffer from any allergies, Mr Prentis?" enquired Shadow.

Neville looked a little startled. "Like the dean, you mean? Marjorie told me what happened. Is that what this is about?"

"We are still making enquiries, but we have reason to believe the wine you bought may be contaminated. As part of our investigation, I'd like to take one of the bottles of Greco Salice Salentino now and arrange to have the council's trading standards officers call to collect the rest of the bottles to be tested."

"But I don't have allergies and what will I tell Marjorie? She'll start asking questions," stammered Neville, who had turned very pale. Shadow, having met Marjorie Prentis, wasn't entirely unsympathetic.

"We'll ask the trading standards team to visit you tomorrow morning while your wife is at work," he said, nodding to Jimmy, who took out his phone to call the council department. "They'll be in an unmarked car, so your neighbours won't have any cause to think anything untoward is happening. How does that sound?"

Neville looked heartbroken, but he nodded his head and reluctantly handed over the bottle of Italian wine.

"Thank you, Chief Inspector. Will I get the bottles back?"

"I'm sorry, I can't promise you that, but if it turns out they aren't contaminated, we might be able to arrange some sort of compensation."

CHAPTER FOUR

Down 6 (7 letters)
If you yell with George, Ann and Rob, you'll have a nasty reaction

HAVING PASSED ON the information to trading standards, the two detectives left Neville in his shed, slumped in his chair, with his head in his hands. They carefully and quietly made their way along the garden path and past the house. Under the cover of darkness, Shadow paused for a second outside the brightly lit sitting room window. Beyond the open door, Marjorie could be seen still talking animatedly on the telephone. As they finally stepped through the garden gate, Jimmy exhaled loudly.

"Poor Mr Prentis. I felt really sorry for him. Imagine being scared of your wife like that."

"It must work for them. There were cards on the sitting room mantelpiece for a pearl wedding anniversary. The Prentises have celebrated thirty years of marriage."

Jimmy shook his head in horror.

"Wow, thirty years! Some people don't get that long for murder! I felt really mean taking his wine away too."

"I know," conceded Shadow, "but it's the only way we can find out what's going on at La Dolce Vita. I'm willing to bet that Woodhouse and Ingham have been putting cheap wine in bottles with more expensive labels and selling it. I think an aficionado like Prentis would have realised it too if he'd actually tasted any of the wine he'd bought. If I'd asked them for any sample bottles, they'd have given us the genuine ones. I imagine the same would have happened if trading standards had called there first."

"You decided to hand the case over to them though, Chief."

"No need to look smug, Sergeant. They are the ones with the power to close La Dolce Vita down or at least seize any more dodgy wine they find."

"Poor Mr Prentis," repeated Jimmy, "even if his bottles turn out to be the real thing, they'll only be able to compensate him with the amount written on his receipt."

"I wonder what Mr Smith thought about Ingham's creative accounting," mused Shadow, half to himself.

At that moment, Jimmy's phone began to bleep. He removed it from his pocket and squinted at the screen in the dark.

"It's forensics. The results on the wine the dean drank are back. They ran tests for peanuts and found a trace," he read.

"A trace? Is that a scientific amount? Is it enough to cause a reaction?" demanded Shadow.

"They don't say, Chief. Maybe it depends how allergic someone is."

"Ask them if they know which grapes were used to make the wine?"

Jimmy tapped rapidly on his phone and waited for the response to ping back.

"Sorry, Chief. They haven't found out yet. They said they'll get back to you."

"What do they do all day?" tutted Shadow. "Tell them we are passing on this case to trading standards; they can liaise with them from now on. Then get Tom to contact the local press. We'll need to put out a warning to anyone else who has bought wine from La Dolce Vita. We can't risk anyone else with a nut allergy drinking from a contaminated bottle," he continued.

"How did the peanuts get in the wine?" asked Jimmy when he'd finished texting and phoning.

"Not peanuts. Peanut oil. You saw what a state the basement was in. Suppose Woodhouse and Ingham happened to use the same funnel they'd used for decanting the peanut oil to pour cheap wine into expensive bottles or whatever they did, without thinking who they could harm. Of course, we can't prove anything until the other bottles have been analysed. But it looks like you and the dean were both right. It was a case of human error, nothing more sinister, nothing to do with the crank sending poison pen letters and nothing worth us investigating."

"We've still got David Smith's death to look into, Chief," replied Jimmy, looking on the bright side as always. "There might still be a connection between him and Woodhouse and Ingham."

Shadow merely grunted in response. They continued walking back down Bootham, moving more quickly than the rush hour traffic that was jammed bumper to bumper. They passed St John's College, one of the city's oldest schools. The lights on the huge Christmas tree twinkled as expensive cars snaked through the gates and lined up to collect the pupils spilling out of the Tudor buildings.

"Maybe we could ask somebody here about Woodhouse and Ingham," suggested Jimmy. "Toby said this is where they met. I remember speaking to the headmaster's secretary during the Susie Slater case and she was really helpful."

"Maybe," replied Shadow, "but Woodhouse and Ingham actually remind me of another case. Do you remember Nick and Andrew, the ghost walkers who were murdered? They had chosen a career that didn't seem to fit their educational backgrounds. Well, Toby and Joe sound the same, especially Joe. Why would someone who has studied the classics, but knows nothing about running a business, open a shop – especially one that doesn't sound like it's making much money."

Jimmy nodded. "Yeh, I remember, Chief. It turned out that Nick and Andrew both had drug convictions."

Before Shadow could reply, Jimmy's phone bleeped

again.

"It's a message from Tom, Chief. He's found out some more information about David Smith. He was a fifty-eight-year-old, self-employed accountant from Leeds. His office is listed as being in Bermuda House on Roseville Road. Tom tried phoning, but there was no answer, not even a machine. Doesn't look like he has any family. Nothing unusual found in his personal effects, only a change of clothes and some toiletries. His wallet had over three hundred quid in cash in it, but no credit or debit cards. There was the bottle of wine. It was about half full and the cork had been jammed back in. He checked with the hotel, La Maison du Fleuve, and they said some of it had been spilt on the carpet in the room. The only weird thing, according to Tom, is that there's no sign of a mobile or laptop. He thought that was odd. It is a bit, isn't it, Chief?"

Shadow nodded as he considered this new information, while Jimmy pondered out loud.

"Why would Toby and Joe use an accountant from Leeds? There must be loads of firms in York," he began, but before Shadow had the chance to reply his sergeant carried on. "Perhaps he was cheap, or perhaps if they issued a lot of dodgy receipts, he was the only one they could find who was prepared to turn a blind eye to what they are getting up to."

"Or maybe he wasn't, and his death wasn't an accident," suggested Shadow thoughtfully.

"You think Toby and Joe were worried he was going to

get them into trouble and they killed him?"

Shadow shook his head as he continued to think.

"It's a bit of a leap from selling dodgy wine and false accounting to murder, but we should pay Messrs Ingham and Woodhouse another visit. Then tomorrow we'll visit the hotel David Smith was found in. Try to arrange a meeting with whoever found the body. Something doesn't add up."

However, by the time they arrived back at La Dolce Vita, the Minster bells were striking five o'clock and the shop was already in darkness. Jimmy tried banging on the door, but there was no sign of life inside.

"It looks like we'll have to come here tomorrow too," Shadow said as they trudged back down the steps. When they arrived back at the station, it seemed strangely quiet.

"Where is everyone?" he asked Tom, who was behind the reception desk.

"There's been an incident down at the coach park," the constable explained. "It sounds like there might have been a bad batch of drugs circulating. We had reports of three people collapsing."

"You see, Chief!" exclaimed Jimmy. "I told you it was only a matter of time before the drug problem in York got worse."

Shadow shook his head. The coach park was notorious. For years, drug users and the city's homeless had congregated there at the benches by the public toilets. Inevitably, every now and then police were called out to deal with an overdose or some other incident. This was nothing new.

"Let me know if you hear anything else?" he called over his shoulder, leaving Jimmy to get the full details from Tom. He made his way up to his office, dodging the tinsel dangling from doorways and the inflatable snowmen that seemed to have sprung up all over the place. He flopped down into the chair at his desk, picked up the piece of paper Jimmy had written Luca's mobile number on and stared at the telephone. The Minster bells were now striking quarter past the hour. It would be after six over in Italy. Would the winery be closed? Perhaps he should wait until tomorrow.

He sat there for nearly ten minutes, thinking about what to say. Luisa's parents had held him responsible for their daughter's death. She should have returned to Italy the week before the accident, but instead she'd stayed with him. When he'd looked in her mother's and father's eyes, he could see what they were thinking. *If it wasn't for you, she would be safe at home with us, not in this coffin.* He didn't blame them. It was only what he thought himself. If he'd encouraged her to go home, she would still be alive. Luca, her brother, had only been a teenager when she'd died. Did he share his parents' opinion? Would he even agree to speak to him? Then he deliberated over using the few Italian phrases he still remembered or should he stick to English and hope whoever answered would understand? Taking a deep breath, he picked up the receiver and dialled the number.

"*Pronto. Luca Greco sono,*" said the voice that answered.

"Hello. This is John Shadow," he began and then immediately wondered if he should have used his title. There was a pause at the other end of the line, then Luca replied in perfect English with only the slightest hint of an American accent.

"Luisa's John?"

Shadow felt his voice catch in his throat. "Yes. It's Luisa's John."

He could hear Luca gasp.

"*Oh Dio*. It is good to hear from you. It has been too long."

"Yes, it has," agreed Shadow as relief swept over him.

"Is it about Luisa?" said the voice at the end of the phone.

"No, Luca, it's about your wine."

He went on to explain what he suspected had happened over the last few days and that they had needed to issue a warning in the local newspaper. Luca was shocked.

"People have become ill drinking my wine? A priest in your cathedral?"

Shadow replied cautiously, knowing he didn't have much evidence to back up his theory. "We think there is a possibility the bottles have been tampered with. Do you recall supplying a shop in York called La Dolce Vita?"

"Yes, yes, I remember. York has always held a special interest for me; since Luisa told me it was your hometown, I wondered if you would return there. I know she hoped to visit it with you one day. So, I know all the businesses we deal with in your city. We supply several restaurants, but this was the first time we had sent our wine to a shop. We sent two crates over."

"So I understand. As I said, we are still running tests. Shall I call you when we have the results?"

"No, John," replied Luca firmly. "I will come over and see what is happening for myself. I will take the next available plane."

"Are you sure?"

"Absolutely – it is the good name of my wine at stake."

Shadow nodded, recalling what Maggie and Gino had both said about how easy it was for a business to be ruined.

"Very well, let me know when you arrive here."

When Shadow had said goodbye, he put the phone back down and stared out of the window for a moment. The bright lights from the hotel opposite were reflecting in the dark swirling water of the River Ouse. Commuters and shoppers hurried over Lendal Bridge on their way to the railway station. Everyday life carried on as normal, yet after speaking to Luca, Shadow felt as if something inside him had changed. There had been a shift. He stood up, pulled on his coat and headed out of the door.

THAT EVENING, LIKE most Mondays, he was dining at La

Scuola Femminile. However, the short walk from St Helen's Square to Petergate seemed to take forever. The St Nicholas Fair was taking place and so the streets were crammed with wooden huts selling Christmas decorations, mince pies, knitted stockings and the dreaded mulled wine. There were also groups of carol singers on every corner. Shadow thought at least he should be grateful that most of them could warble away in tune. Although it was quite early when he finally arrived at the restaurant, the place seemed busier than usual with Francesco, the owner, and his son, Marco, hurrying back and forth to the kitchen.

"Christmas parties?" enquired Shadow, nodding towards the large groups at the other tables. The men were loosening their ties and putting paper crowns on their heads while the women pulled crackers and sipped Prosecco.

"Yes, we're fully booked," explained Marco as he placed the bottle of Greco Salice Salentino on Shadow's table, "and short-staffed. One of the waitresses hasn't turned up for her shift. Mum was planning on having a night off, but Dad's phoned and asked her to come in. She won't be happy."

The young man hurried away, checking on tables as he went. Shadow studied the bottle before lifting the glass and inhaling deeply and tentatively taking a sip. He was relieved to find it was the real thing. Marco returned a few minutes later with a plate of garlic bread and linguine amatriciana. Unfortunately, despite the food and wine being delicious, Shadow found he wasn't enjoying it as much as usual. The noisy chatter and shrieks of festive laughter from the other tables were beginning to grate. He kept his head lowered and quickly finished his meal. Then he paid the bill and left as a barrage of party poppers were being let off.

However, having only taken a few steps along Petergate, he realised bolting down his food and wine may have been a mistake. His stomach certainly seemed to think so. Despite much rummaging he was unable to locate any indigestion tablets, nor could he recall having any back on *Florence*. With a sigh of resignation, he turned up the collar of his coat against the biting wind and went in search of a late-night chemist. He finally found one on Lendal. Blinking as he stepped from the dark street into the harsh bright lights, he was greeted by a small man with a neatly trimmed beard wearing a white coat. Shadow selected his preferred brand of tablets from the selection on the counter, then went to pay. As he handed over his money, he noticed the name tag on the pharmacist's coat: Ranjiv Patel. He recalled his earlier conversation with Joe Ingham. Glancing over his shoulder, he could see the metal archway that led down to Lendal Cellars and La Dolce Vita. Turning back to Mr Patel, he nodded at the sign taped to the till showing the opening times. Seven days a week, from eight in the morning until ten at night.

"You certainly work long hours," he commented.

Mr Patel shrugged. "I believe it is important to provide a service to our community. I like to think we are here when our customers need us. Besides, these days it is not as hard as when it was only me and my wife. Two years ago, our son joined us and this summer, my daughter became a qualified pharmacist too. It's turning into a real family business. There is always one of us here. We may even need to find a second shop," he explained with a hint of pride in his voice.

"I suppose the upside of always being here is you never miss a delivery."

"No never. Indeed, we often find ourselves taking in parcels for our neighbours."

"I'm sure they appreciate it, particularly those that don't open so early. I was in La Dolce Vita this morning and noticed they don't open until ten thirty."

Mr Patel's forehead creased. "Oh yes, the two young men who have opened next door to the Cellars. We did take a delivery for them. It was a few weeks ago now and only a small parcel. My wife took it round."

"That was kind of her."

"It was, but they were quite rude to her. She found them in the storeroom beneath the shop and one of them accused her of sneaking up on them. Not a word of thanks."

"Some people," tutted Shadow with a shake of his head. He accepted his change from Mr Patel and wished him a good evening as he left.

He plodded down Coney Street, letting a chalky tablet dissolve in his mouth and trying to ignore the Christmas lights and the late-night shoppers. While he was deep in thought, his ears were suddenly assaulted be a loud, tuneless rendition of "We Wish You a Merry Christmas". He stopped by a shop doorway. Jamie, a young man with more tattoos than teeth and one of the city's regular rough sleepers, was slumped inside, an empty paper cup optimistically placed in front of him.

"Are you on your own tonight?" he asked.

Jamie was rarely seen without his girlfriend.

"Kayleigh's still in hospital, isn't she," replied the young man warily.

"What happened to her?"

"She had a bad trip."

"Down at the coach park?" asked Shadow, wondering if she was one of those uniform had dealt with earlier.

"That's right. There's some dodgy coke about."

"You didn't take any?"

"Not me, Mr Shadow, I'm clean," replied Jamie with a crooked grin.

"Of course you are," muttered Shadow.

Jamie began singing again. Shadow bent down and stuck a ten-pound note in his cup. He paused when he noticed it was from La Dolce Vita.

"Did someone buy you a coffee?"

"Not me, I hate the stuff. Some tall, skinny bloke gave it to Kayleigh. I only drink tea, me."

"Well go and buy yourself a cup now and find yourself somewhere warm to sleep. And for crying out loud, learn the second verse," Shadow called over his shoulder as he walked away.

A frost was already glinting on the grass verge as he walked along the towpath where *Florence* was moored. His arrival was welcomed by the noisy honking of his neighbours, the geese, who had settled on his roof. When on board, he shrugged off his coat and shivered. He briefly considered lighting the small, wood-burning stove in the sitting area of the boat, but instead decided to turn in for the night. He flopped into bed and turned his head to look at Luisa's photo next to his bed. Smiling as she sat on the roof of *Florence*, shielding her eyes from the sun, she seemed frozen in time. They had only spent one Christmas together, but it was the happiest he'd known. It had felt strange to speak to Luca, her brother, after all these years. To connect to someone who remembered Luisa as clearly as he did.

He thumped his pillow and closed his eyes, but he couldn't seem to settle. What Luca had said was true. He and Luisa had planned to visit York together. Perhaps it was a blessing they had never made it. After he'd lost her, he couldn't bear to stay in London, expecting to see her whenever he heard light, quick footsteps on the towpath by the Regent's Canal. He and *Florence* had headed north to his home city, which held many memories but none of Luisa.

Frustrated, he pummelled his pillow again. Then, in the distance, he began to hear the faint sound of sirens. He listened, but they didn't fade away, instead they seemed to be getting closer. Flinging back his duvet he got out of bed and peered through the curtains. There was an ominous blue glow coming from further down the river. Then, right on cue, his phone began to ring.

"Yes, Sergeant?"

"Oh, hi, Chief. Are you awake?" said Jimmy at the other end of the line.

"Obviously," sighed Shadow. "What have you got to tell me?"

"We've got a body, Chief. They've just pulled her out of the river under Lendal Bridge."

"All right, I'm on my way."

He put the phone down and a few minutes later, he was dressed once more. He paused as he pulled on his jacket and peered out of the window. The icy towpath was glistening in the moonlight. Walking down to Lendal Bridge would take at least twenty minutes and he'd be freezing by the time he got there, so instead he made his way out to the stern deck and leaned across to untie the mooring rope. Then he started the engine and, with a gloved hand resting on the tiller, steered *Florence* down the river, under Skeldergate Bridge and Ouse Bridge towards the blue flashing lights.

Five minutes later, he moored *Florence* a few yards away from Lendal Bridge, then stepped on to the path and made his way to where his colleagues were congregated. He nodded to the paramedics, who were standing by the trolley holding the body and talking to Sophie. She turned when she heard his footsteps.

"Hi, Chief. Would you like to have a look before they take her away?"

"I suppose so," replied Shadow.

One of the paramedics raised the plastic sheet. Shadow took a deep breath and steeled himself. When he looked at the body, the first thing he noticed was a mass of long, blonde hair. Wet and matted, it was sticking to the young woman's face. Although, it was now bloated and discoloured, it had clearly once been beautiful. She was still dressed in a simple, short black dress with thin shoulder straps and there was a small tattoo of a butterfly on her upper left arm. Her feet were still encased in a pair of black high heels. His eyes lingered on a deep, ugly injury to her right ankle above the buckle of the shoe strap. Sophie followed his gaze.

"A stone had been tied to her ankle to weigh her down, but the rope must have either broken or maybe it was eaten by something. It's all been bagged up for forensics to take a look at," she explained.

"So she didn't fall in then?" queried Shadow. From the way she was dressed he had wondered if she could have been a drunken reveller who had taken a tumble. She wouldn't have been the first, but a weight around the ankle pointed to her dying at someone else's hand. "Any other signs of injury?" he asked, nodding to the paramedics again, who lowered the sheet once more.

"She'd received a pretty hefty blow to the back of her

head by the look of things, but I'll be able to tell you more later."

At that moment, Jimmy – who had been talking to the dive team – came hurrying over.

"Evening, Chief, or should I say, morning? Well, as you can see, she's a white female in her early twenties," he began. Shadow grunted impatiently and turned his attention back to Sophie.

"How long has she been in there?"

"A few days at the most, certainly not more than a week," she replied.

"Can you tell if she'd taken anything?"

"There are no signs of needle marks on her arms, but I won't know for definite until after the post-mortem."

"Okay, thanks, Sophie," said Shadow.

"Goodnight, Chief. See you later, Jimmy," replied Sophie with a wave as she followed the paramedics, who were wheeling the body away to the waiting ambulance.

"Have we any idea who she was?" asked Shadow. Jimmy shook his head and gestured towards the dive team, who were beginning to pack up their equipment.

"There was no ID on her and no sign of a handbag or purse down there either. They did find a black puffa-style jacket, caught up in some weeds. We think that might be hers. There were some keys in the pocket, but nothing else. I'll start checking missing persons as soon as I get back to the office."

"I've told you. It's Anna," said a gruff voice behind them. Shadow turned to find Jake, another of the city's rough sleepers, leaning against the wall beneath the bridge. Missy, his spaniel, was sitting by his feet. Her eyes were fixed on Jake, but she was unusually subdued. The two of them had been living on the street for years.

"Jake made the call to us, Chief," Jimmy began to explain, but Shadow interrupted him.

"Anna who?" he asked.

Jake shrugged. His hand shook as he took a drag on his cigarette.

"I don't know her second name. She moved to York about a year ago, but she was from Slovenia. She used to walk along here by the river most days."

The three of them stopped to watch as the ambulance, its lights no longer flashing, was driven away through the crowd of late-night revellers who had gathered on the other side of the bridge, straining their necks to see what was going on.

"We'll need you to make a statement," said Jimmy.

Jake glared at him. "I'm not going to the station," he declared defiantly.

"Well, it's too cold to talk out here," said Shadow turning up the collar of his jacket. "Do you have any objections to talking to us on my boat?"

Jake looked at him warily as he took another drag. "Missy too?"

"Naturally," agreed Shadow.

"All right."

Jake collected up his rolled-up sleeping bag and rucksack, then the three men and the spaniel made their way along the path towards *Florence*. They had almost reached the boat when there was a flash of light and the sound of running feet behind them.

"Chief Inspector Shadow, do you have a comment for the readers of the *Herald*?" shouted out a loud, Scottish voice. Shadow groaned. Kevin MacNab, the journalist he had managed to dodge earlier. He looked over his shoulder to see the red-haired reporter along with an equally eager photographer.

"No, I don't," he snapped as the camera flashed again, causing Missy to start barking erratically.

"Have you identified the body yet? Is someone helping you with your inquires?" persisted MacNab.

"A statement will be released in due course," said Jimmy diplomatically as they reached *Florence*. When they were all aboard, Jake took a seat on the edge of one of the sofas. Missy sniffed all the furniture suspiciously, before turning in a circle three times and finally settling at Jake's feet. Shadow lit the wood-burning stove and Jimmy clattered around in the galley as he made coffee for them all.

"So how do you know Anna?" asked Shadow, settling down on the sofa opposite Jake.

The younger man wrapped his hands around his mug of coffee and took a sip before answering. "Like I said, she used to walk by the river most days. She was nice. She didn't ignore us or act like we weren't there, not like most people. She would always stop to say 'hello' and make a fuss of Missy."

The dog wagged her tail at the mention of her name, as if to confirm Jake's story.

"When did you last see her?"

"A few days ago, I asked her if she was going home for Christmas, but she said no, she was staying here working extra shifts, covering for everyone else who didn't want to work. She was a real grafter. She had about three jobs and she was studying English too."

Jake's smile faded and he ran a hand across his unshaven chin.

"It was the full moon, you see," he continued. "It was shining right on the water. That's when I saw her. It was her hair. She had really lovely, long blonde hair. Natural too, not bleached. All I could see was the hair, floating below the surface. I knew it was her. The water was moving quickly, but she must have been tangled up in the weeds or some-thing because it didn't carry her away. I thought about jumping in, but I knew the current was too strong." He took another sip of coffee. "That's when I called you lot out."

"Have you got a phone?" asked Jimmy in surprise. He was perched at the small, fold-down dining table, taking notes. Shadow and Jake both turned and scowled at him.

"Yeh, I've got a phone," Jake replied defensively. "One of

the charities gives them out with enough credit to last a month. So what? It's a necessity, not a luxury these days. I only use it to call one of the hostels and find out if they've got a room for the night or for emergencies like tonight."

"I was only asking," murmured Jimmy as Shadow continued to frown. He was more interested in what Jake had to say about the dead girl than his means of communication.

"You said she was from Slovenia. Do you know anything else about her? Her age? Address? Did she have a boyfriend?"

Jake shook his head. "No, sometimes she talked about her family. She missed them, especially her little sister, but mainly we talked about books." He looked up and gave Shadow a half-smile. "This'll give you a laugh. We both liked detective stories." Shadow didn't laugh, he simply listened as Jake continued to speak.

"She saw me reading an old Ruth Rendell one day and asked if I was enjoying it."

He paused as if lost in his thoughts. Missy whined quietly.

"You said she walked along the river every day. Where was she going?" asked Shadow.

"She worked in that new flash hotel on the other side of the river. You know the one with the rooftop bar? She mainly worked nights, so she used to pass by in the evenings."

"La Maison du Fleuve," interrupted Jimmy, earning himself another scowl.

"Do you know where else she worked?"

"She had a cleaning job in the mornings, then did a lunchtime shift as a waitress in one of the restaurants. A couple of afternoons a week, she took English lessons. Like I said, she was a real grafter."

Jake drank down the last of his coffee and rose to his feet.

"It wasn't an accident, was it?" he asked softly.

Shadow shook his head. "No, we don't think it was."

Jake hauled his sleeping bag and rucksack on his back and looked Shadow straight in the eye.

"You will catch the bastard, won't you, Shadow?"

"Yes, I will," replied Shadow, standing up to shake his hand.

"Are you heading back to the bridge?" asked Jimmy. "It's just that I'll need to print off this statement and get a signature."

"I'm not signing anything," said Jake, heading towards the door with Missy at his heels. "I won't be able to sleep. We're going for a walk until the Salvation Army opens for breakfast at six. You can find me there if you need me, but I'm signing nothing."

A cold gust of wind blew into the boat as Jake and Missy stepped out into the dark, Jake closing the door loudly behind them.

"I do wish you wouldn't interrupt witnesses. I must have told you a million times," grumbled Shadow.

"Sorry, Chief, but the hotel she worked in was the same

as the one Smith the accountant was staying in. I thought it might be important."

"Well, yes it might be," admitted Shadow, slightly mollified, "but let's find out exactly who she was and how long she's been in the river before we jump to any conclusions."

"So, what next, Chief?" asked Jimmy. Shadow looked at his watch and yawned.

"Well, I don't know about you, Sergeant, but I'm going to attempt to get a couple of hours' sleep. I would suggest you do the same."

CHAPTER FIVE

Down 4 (8 letters)
Treat hen kindly; don't scare her

WHEN SHADOW ARRIVED at the police station the next morning, Jimmy was already waiting for him outside his office door.

"Found her, Chief. Anna Novak, Slovenian national, twenty-three years old, reported missing yesterday."

"Who reported her missing?"

"Actually, it was Lucia," said Jimmy.

Shadow looked at him in surprise. "Lucia from La Scuola Femminile? Francesco's wife?"

"Yes, Chief. She filed the report late last night. It seems Anna was a waitress there. Remember Jake said she worked in a restaurant? She didn't turn up for her shift or answer her phone when Lucia called. Apparently, this was very out of character, so when the restaurant had closed, Lucia and Marco went to check where she lived. They knocked on her door, but there was no sign of her, so they came here to the station."

Shadow nodded, recalling Marco telling him they were

short-staffed the previous night.

"Have you got Anna's address?" he asked.

"Yes, Chief. She rented a flat on Ogleforth. The building's owned by the church, but I've got the set of keys from the jacket that the dive team found. I thought we'd try those."

"Right, let's go and take a look and tell Tom to contact the Slovenian police, so they can inform her family."

OGLEFORTH WAS A narrow, cobbled street that led from the back of the Minster to Goodramgate. Like many of the streets in the city, several of the buildings there were owned by the Church of England. However, unlike many of the streets it was empty of tourists, who – distracted by either the Minster or Treasurer's House – missed the discreet entrance. The footsteps of the two detectives echoed as they headed to the address Jimmy had found.

Anna's flat was in a tall, thin Victorian building. Shadow noted it was opposite a similar building that housed the administrative offices for the Minster, where Marjorie Prentis worked. Both detectives slipped on a pair of protective gloves, then Jimmy unlocked the glossy, black front door with a Yale key. He glanced at the piece of paper in his hand.

"Anna lived in flat nine, Chief. That's on the top floor," he said.

"Of course it is and I bet there isn't a lift," complained Shadow as he began trudging up the steep, narrow stairs behind his more sprightly sergeant. At the top, he paused to catch his breath for a moment outside the door marked with the number nine, while Jimmy tried each of the other two keys on the chain to find the correct one. When the two detectives stepped inside, they found it was really more of a bedsit than a flat. It was a tiny room with a sloping ceiling. There was a single bed, a table with two chairs, a couple of cupboards and a sink in one corner with a small hob set into the worktop. A folding door in the other corner led to a compact shower room. Even his own bathroom on *Florence* was more spacious, Shadow thought as he opened the mirrored cabinet crammed with cosmetics and beauty products.

He stepped back into the main room and looked around. Although it was small, Anna had clearly tried her best to make it feel homely. The bed had a purple duvet cover and was scattered with pink and purple cushions. There was a mirror in the shape of a butterfly and fairy lights were draped around a pinboard on the wall. Jimmy was standing at the window.

"If you tilt your head to the left, you get a really good view of the Minster," he said thoughtfully.

Shadow shook his head in despair. "That would be wonderful if we were a pair of estate agents trying to sell the place. Now let's see if we can find something more useful,

Sergeant. You start in that chest of drawers."

"Okay, Chief," replied Jimmy as he pulled open the first drawer, "but I hate doing this. It always feels like we are intruding. I can't help thinking Anna wouldn't want two strange men going through all her stuff. Look, all her underwear is in here."

"I don't think she'd mind, if it helps us catch whoever killed her."

Shadow glanced around. Jake had said Anna was an avid reader, but there was only one book on the bedside table. It was a hardback copy of the latest Robert Galbraith novel. Shadow picked it up and looked inside. It was a copy from York library. Anna had borrowed it almost a week ago. She had been using a folded copy of the library newsletter as a bookmark.

"I've found her diary," announced Jimmy.

"And?" enquired Shadow, glancing across to his sergeant, who was flicking through a notebook decorated with pink and purple butterflies.

"It looks like she mainly used it to keep track of when and where she was working. She used abbreviations. At noon most days she's written SF, that must be La Scuola Femminile, MdF must be La Maison du Fleuve, the hotel Jake said she worked nights at. Then there's DV. I wonder what that stands for?"

"No wonder she needed a diary to keep track of everything. She must have been exhausted," murmured Shadow as he put the book back down. Then a thought occurred to him. "DV? Didn't Ingham say their cleaner hadn't turned up that morning?"

"Yes, Chief. DV, La Dolce Vita. It would fit," replied Jimmy excitedly. "Another connection to Woodhouse and Ingham. Should we go and speak to them?"

"No, not yet. I want to go and speak to Lucia first. You track Jake down too, see if Anna ever said anything about La Dolce Vita to him. Any mention of a boyfriend in there?"

"Not a name, but it's quite sweet – she's drawn a little heart next to some dates and times. Usually Friday afternoons."

"Locations?"

"No, sorry, Chief. Maybe they always met at the same place, so she didn't need to write it down."

"Maybe. Assuming she disappeared sometime over the weekend, is there any mention of her meeting anyone on Saturday or Sunday?"

"No, it's mainly details of where and when she was working, but there's a bit of scribbling out. It looks like she was trying to rearrange her shifts for yesterday."

Shadow grunted in response. He was standing in front of Anna's pinboard. It was mainly covered with photographs of Anna and what he assumed was her family. There was a picture of Anna with her parents and a smaller version of herself, the little sister Jake had told them about. She had certainly been a striking young woman. Even without a formal identification there was now no doubt the body they had recovered was her. Shadow sighed to himself. Only twenty-three years old. The same age Luisa was when she'd died. At least Luisa's death had been an accident; someone hadn't violently ended her life on purpose.

"That's weird!" exclaimed Jimmy suddenly.

"What is?" asked Shadow as he carefully removed a photo of Anna on her own from the board and slipped it into his pocket.

"Look, Chief, she's written your name."

Shadow walked over and studied the page Jimmy was holding open. There it was quite clearly. *Chief Inspector Shadow* written in the young woman's neatly curved handwriting. The entry was for the previous evening and was next to the letters SF.

"That's for last night. The shift she didn't turn up for," he said. "It looks like she was originally meant to be working at lunchtime, but swapped shifts to the evening instead. Perhaps she knew I usually dine there on a Monday and wanted to speak to me."

Jimmy nodded. "That makes sense, Chief."

"Well, I think it sounds very fishy," said a voice behind them. Both detectives jumped and turned around to see Marjorie Prentis watching them with her arms folded and a look of disapproval on her face. "And what do you both think you're doing poking around in Anna's things. What's she been up to?"

"I'm sorry to inform you that we have reason to believe Miss Novak may be dead," replied Shadow.

Marjorie showed no sign of surprise or shock but narrowed her eyes suspiciously. "Was it drugs?"

"What makes you say that?"

Marjorie shrugged. "Well, she was only young and she looked healthy enough, but she was a bit on the skinny side. You can't always tell, can you? And only last night there was a report in the *Herald* about all those druggies in the coach park needing to be taken to hospital. Wasting NHS resources on the likes of them. It's taxpayers like me who have to foot the bill. They should have been left there. That would teach them not to mess about with drugs."

"Miss Novak was reported missing and a body matching her description was recovered from the river early this morning."

"How did she end up there?"

Shadow didn't answer the question.

"When did you last see her?" he asked instead.

Marjorie shrugged again. "I can't remember when I last spoke to her, but she was here late on Sunday afternoon. We were taking the orders of service for the Advent ceremony from the office over to the Minster at about five-ish. I happened to look up and she was closing her curtains."

Shadow nodded. "Was she alone?"

"How am I supposed to know? I only saw her for a second."

"Did you know her well?"

"Not really."

"Would you say she was a good tenant?"

"Yes, she was," conceded Marjorie, a little reluctantly. "Clean, tidy, polite, she always paid her rent on time and no parties or loud music blaring out like some of our younger tenants."

"I see. Well, thank you for your time, Mrs Prentis. You have been very helpful."

Pursing her lips, Marjorie nodded. "All right, but before you leave, I want you to come to the office and sign something to say you've been rummaging around up here. This is Minster property. If anything of Anna's has gone missing, I don't want to be held responsible."

"As you wish, Mrs Prentis," replied Shadow as Marjorie stomped back down the stairs.

"Poor Mr Prentis," murmured Jimmy, who had been rapidly noting down everything Marjorie had told them. "She's a nightmare!"

"Yes," agreed Shadow, "but useful. Now we know Anna was probably killed sometime on Sunday evening and before she was due at La Dolce Vita on Monday morning, assuming that is what DV stands for."

They spent another half an hour looking through Anna's belongings but found little more of interest. They left the flat and knocked on the doors of each of Anna's neighbours, but nobody appeared to be at home. When they stepped back out on to the cobbled street, the twitching curtains in the offices across the road told Shadow that Mrs Prentis was watching and waiting for him.

"You get back to the station and see what forensics and Sophie have to report," said Shadow. "Hopefully, she'll be able to confirm the time of death. Then try to arrange a visit to that hotel so we can see if there is any connection between Smith and Anna."

"Okay, Chief. Where are you going?" asked Jimmy.

"To break the news about Anna to Lucia and Francesco. As soon as I can escape from here, that is." He pushed open the office door and entered Marjorie's lair. He quickly scribbled his signature on the sheaf of papers she had waiting for him and was about to leave again when she stopped him.

"Not so fast! There's something else, while you are here. I've got the paperwork for that wine that made the dean ill." Marjorie pushed another piece of paper across the desk. "Look there, you can see it was signed by Canon Marchman. It had nothing to do with me. That's a photocopy for you. Take it with you and make sure you file it away properly."

"Thank you, Mrs Prentis," replied Shadow politely as he folded the sheet of paper and slipped it into his pocket, although in truth he hadn't given the wine much thought since they'd discovered Anna's body.

THE MINSTER BELLS were striking eleven o'clock as he left the offices and headed down Ogleforth, to Goodramgate, then on to Petergate. When Shadow arrived outside La Scuola Femminile, Marco was opening the door.

"Hello, Chief Inspector," he said politely. "I wasn't expecting to see you again so soon and we don't usually see you at lunchtime. The kitchen isn't quite open yet, but I'm sure we can rustle you something up."

"That's kind, Marco, but no thank you," replied Shadow. "Unfortunately, this isn't a social call. Are your mum and dad around? I'd like to speak to them before your customers start to arrive."

Looking worried, Marco led Shadow into the private dining room at the back of the restaurant. A few moments later, Lucia came hurrying in, looking anxious as she wiped her hands on a striped cloth.

"Marco said you wanted to talk to me. I'm sorry, but Francesco is out at the wholesaler's. Is something wrong, Chief Inspector?"

Shadow pulled a chair out for her.

"Yes, Lucia. Perhaps you should sit down. I'm afraid I have some bad news."

Lucia obediently took a seat as Shadow cleared his throat.

"Late last night, you reported that Anna Novak, one of your employees, was missing."

"Oh Anna is more than an employee. She has only been

with us a few months, but she was like one of the family. Has something happened to her?"

Shadow nodded slowly. He hated this part of his job. Even after all these years, it never got any easier.

"I'm very sorry, Lucia, but we think Anna is dead. We found the body of a young woman in the river in the early hours of this morning. No formal identification has been made, but the body does match Anna's description."

Lucia's hand flew to her mouth and her eyes filled with tears. Marco, who had been hovering in the doorway, hurried forward and wrapped his arms around his mother.

"I'm sorry," repeated Shadow, awkwardly handing his handkerchief to Lucia, who was now sobbing loudly.

"What happened?" asked Marco.

"We don't know yet," replied Shadow. "Can you tell me when you last saw her?"

Marco nodded. "Yes, it was on Saturday. She finished her shift at two thirty, as usual. She said goodbye and confirmed she would be working on Monday night instead of at lunchtime. Looking back, I guess she was a bit quiet."

"I knew something was wrong," interrupted Lucia between sobs. "I should have asked Francesco to speak to you as soon as she didn't turn up, Chief Inspector. She was never late, never."

"How long had she been working here? I don't recall ever seeing her," asked Shadow.

"She normally only worked lunchtime shifts," explained

Marco, "but she'd been here since the end of summer. Dad will have the exact date if you need it."

"Thank you – that would be helpful," replied Shadow.

Lucia reached out and took his hand. "After her shift, she would sometimes stay in the kitchen for a bite to eat and a chat. She spoke Italian like one of us. Then she would dash off again. She had so many jobs I couldn't keep track of her. On her feet here and all night at that hotel. Then up early to clean up after those two messy young men."

"Do you mean Joseph Ingham and Toby Woodhouse at La Dolce Vita?" queried Shadow.

"Hah, La Dolce Vita!" tutted Lucia, her expression telling Shadow exactly what she thought of the place. "Anna was wasted there. She was such a good girl, working hard and sending money home."

Tears began rolling down her face again, but Shadow pressed on, wanting to get the interview over with as soon as possible. He hated seeing Lucia and her son so upset.

"There is something else I would like to ask you about. We found her diary and my name was written in it. Had she ever mentioned me to you?"

Lucia looked up and wiped her eyes. "It was me who mentioned you to her, Chief Inspector. Let me explain." She took a deep breath to try to compose herself. "Anna had been very quiet on Friday. I asked her if something was wrong and she said she was worried. She thought someone had done something bad, but she wasn't sure and didn't want to get anyone into trouble. I asked if she meant bad like a crime, and she said yes. So, I told her she should go to the police, but she shook her head. She looked scared. I asked her if she was frightened of being seen going to the police station. She nodded and looked like she was going to cry. That's when I told her about you. I told her which nights you usually come here and that if she was here, I was sure you would speak to her privately and nobody would ever have to know."

"And she liked that idea?" asked Shadow.

"Oh yes, she seemed very relieved. That's when she asked to change her shift from Monday lunchtime to Monday evening. So, you see when Francesco called me and said she hadn't come in I sensed straightaway something was wrong. I hoped you would still be here, so I could talk to you, but you had left already, and we were so busy…" She trailed off and began sobbing again. Shadow stood up.

"Please, Lucia, you must not blame yourself," he said, patting her awkwardly on the shoulder. Then he turned to Marco and lowered his voice. "We are trying to contact Anna's family, but if for any reason they aren't able to come over, we may need someone who knew her to identify the body."

The young man nodded.

"It might be better to ask Dad," said Marco. "I'm sure he'll do it if you need him to."

"Of course," agreed Shadow. "You stay with her, Marco. I'll see myself out."

BACK AT THE station, Shadow found Jimmy in the incident room that had been set up.

"Hi, Chief. How did Lucia take the news?" he asked.

"How do you think?" replied Shadow, removing the photo of Anna from his pocket and attaching it to one of the whiteboards. "What have you got to tell me?"

"Sophie has finished the post-mortem. She hasn't written a full report yet, but she phoned through with the main points." Jimmy consulted his electronic notebook and began to scroll through. "Anna didn't have any drugs or alcohol in her system. No underlying health conditions. She'd been in the water for about twenty-four hours, which fits in with what we already know. She'd suffered a blow to the back of her skull, but no other injuries except for where the rope had been tied around her ankle. No signs of sexual assault. When she went into the water, she was alive but unconscious."

"Have forensics been able to tell us anything about the rope and stone?" asked Shadow.

Jimmy shook his head. "Not yet, Chief. They are running a bit late. They went to hand over the wine they'd been testing to trading standards, who were in turn running late after going to collect the wine from Mr Prentis."

Shadow sat down with a sigh. "I'd forgotten about that. How did it go?"

Jimmy pulled a face. "Not great, Chief. The poor guy

staged a bit of a protest."

"What do you mean?"

"He'd locked himself in the shed and had drunk a bottle and a half of wine by the time they got there. One of the trading standards guys called uniform out. They were worried Neville would hurt himself. They managed to get in and trading standards said they should still be able to test the empty bottle."

"What about Mr Prentis?"

"He was crying quite a bit, then he was sick. The constable gave him some water and he seemed to sober up a bit. Poor guy. His wife's bound to find out what he's been up to now."

"It sounds like quite an eventful morning," replied Shadow. "Get in touch with Ben and Ollie to try to get them to hurry up with the rope and stone. We'll all have to leave this business with the wine to trading standards now. Besides, with any luck, Luca will be able to tell us if there is anything we need to know when he arrives and looks at the bottle we took from Neville."

"You must be looking forward to seeing him after all this time, Chief."

Shadow was saved from having to answer by Jimmy's phone bleeping.

"Anything useful, Sergeant?"

"Yes, I contacted La Maison du Fleuve, the hotel where David Smith was found and where Anna worked. I told them what had happened to her. She worked there every night except Sundays but had asked to change her shift on Monday night. They said they would call in the night manager so we could speak to him."

"Good. When?"

"He's there now, Chief."

"Then let's head over there. By the way, Lucia said Anna was worried about something. She thought someone might have committed a crime and said she wanted to speak to me. That's why she changed her shift to Monday night. Unfortunately, it was too late. Lucia also confirmed Anna was the cleaner at La Dolce Vita."

"So do you think Ingham and Woodhouse are involved in all this?"

Shadow shook his head. "I really don't know. At the moment, the more information we receive the less clear everything becomes."

IT WAS BEGINNING to snow as they arrived at the Maison du Fleuve hotel. The hotel was a large concrete and glass structure, situated on the opposite side of the river to Shadow's office in the medieval Guildhall. It had been built in the 1980s to house the offices of one of the many insurance companies that made York their home. Recently, it had been turned into a chic boutique hotel. The locals joked that it should be called the Maison du Flood due to its proximity to the river. However, it had proved to be very popular with the city's young and fashionable visitors, due partly to its large rooftop bar that provided guests with a long cocktail list and incredible views.

The two detectives stepped into the hotel reception. It was dimly lit and decorated in various hues of grey and white with glass and polished cement flooring and furniture. The centre of the room was dominated by a huge black and silver Christmas tree. Shadow didn't think it looked remotely festive. There was also hip-hop music playing in the background that Jimmy immediately started nodding his head in time to as they waited for a group of Chinese tourists to check in.

When they had finished, the elegant young lady in the smart black trouser suit behind the reception desk turned her attention to Shadow and Jimmy, but her bright smile soon disappeared when the two detectives introduced themselves. She quickly ushered them through a door marked "private – staff only" and away from some more guests who were waiting to check out. They followed her down a long corridor.

"Did you know Anna Novak?" asked Jimmy.

"No," she replied bluntly. "We never worked together."

A few seconds later, she came to a halt outside a door marked "Night Manager".

"Craig Philips, our night manager, is waiting for you in

his office," she said in hushed tones. "This is the key for the penthouse, where Mr Smith was found. It has been deep-cleaned but we are still waiting for the carpet to be replaced before we can let another guest stay there," she explained, handing a key with a velvet tassel to Jimmy, "and we would appreciate it if you could be as discreet as possible during your time at the Maison du Fleuve," she finished with a tight smile.

Then she gave the office door a brisk knock, turned on her heel and marched back down the corridor as a voice from behind the door called out, "Yes?"

Shadow and Jimmy stepped inside and found the night manager slumped at his desk in the small, untidy office. He was in his thirties, unshaven, with hollow eyes, and he didn't bother standing up when the two detectives entered the room.

"If this is about that bloke who hit his head and died, you're wasting your time," he said before Shadow even had chance to open his mouth. "I can't be held responsible for every idiot who goes and falls over."

"It wasn't only Mr Smith's death we wanted to discuss with you, Mr Philips. We also wanted to speak to you about Anna Novak."

The night manager exhaled slowly and Shadow thought he caught a faint whiff of whisky.

"Yes, I heard about that. It's a shame. She was a nice girl and a real looker too. The waiters and all the guys in the kitchen tried it on with her, a few of the guests as well, but she wasn't interested. Said she had a boyfriend, not that we ever saw her with anyone."

Shadow wondered if the night manager had been rebuffed too.

"Did she mention her boyfriend's name at all?" asked Jimmy, who as usual was engrossed with entering all the details into his electronic notebook.

"No. For all I know it was some lad back home in…" he paused "…wherever it was she came from."

"Slovenia," provided Jimmy.

"Slovenia, Slovakia, it's all the same to me. It's like the United Nations here. We've got staff from all over the place. Poles, Portuguese, Bulgarians, Romanians. I can't be expected to keep track of them all."

"What did Anna do here?" asked Shadow.

"She was a waitress. It was her job to take room service orders, pass them on to the kitchen, then deliver the trays to the right room. She always worked the night shift, six nights a week, seven pm to one am – that's when the kitchens close."

"What night didn't she work?"

"Sundays, except for this week when she switched with one of the other girls who worked on Monday."

"So she was working on Sunday night?"

"Yes, like I said seven until one," replied Philips with a yawn.

"And she was working here on Thursday, the night David Smith died?"

"Yes, it was Anna who found him."

Shadow looked up with interest. "What happened exactly?"

"He'd phoned down an order. Fillet steak and chips, if I remember correctly. Anna took the order, then took the tray up. She said she knocked but there was no answer. She waited, knocked again, called out his name. There wasn't a 'do not disturb' sign on the door, so she used her master key to let herself in. She assumed he was in the shower or something and planned to leave it for him; instead she found the bathroom door open and him sprawled out on the floor."

"Had she been up earlier to take him the bottle of wine or was that one of the bar staff?" asked Shadow, wondering if Joe Ingham had been telling them the truth about giving a bottle to the accountant.

Philips shook his head. "No, that wine he was drinking isn't one we stock. I don't know where he got it from. We don't encourage it, but we can't stop guests bringing their own wine or food in and there are corkscrews and glasses provided next to the minibar in all the rooms."

"Was Anna upset about finding Mr Smith?" asked Jimmy.

Philips looked at him incredulously. "Of course she was. Nobody likes to find a dead body, do they? I sent her home early. What's all this about anyway?"

Shadow ignored him and carried on with his own questions. "Were you particularly busy that night?"

"Yeh, it was manic. We were fully booked. The restaurant was packed with Christmas parties. We had to take extra staff on to keep the rooftop bar going."

"Did Mr Smith have any visitors that evening?"

"None who signed in at reception." Philips yawned again.

"One more question?" said Shadow. "All the staff we've seen so far, both male and female, are wearing black trouser suits. Is that the hotel's uniform?"

"Yeh, we all wear the same. Waitresses, porters, bar staff. Management think it helps us blend in with the guests, create a more cohesive atmosphere, whatever that means."

"I see; well, thank you for your time, Mr Philips. We're going to take a look at the penthouse. Would you mind waiting here in case we have any questions afterwards?"

Philips grunted as he let his head loll back against his chair.

"I don't suppose I've got much choice. It doesn't look like be catching up on any sleep today, does it?"

Shadow thanked the night manager again and together he and Jimmy left the office and walked back down the corridor until they returned to the reception area, entered the lift and hit the button for the top floor.

"Do you think Anna wanted to talk to you about finding the body?" asked Jimmy as soon as the lift door slid shut.

"Maybe she didn't think it was an accident either."

They stepped out of the lift and made their way to the penthouse. Shadow noticed they were being watched by a petite dark-haired maid at the end of the corridor. He nodded politely towards her, but she quickly ducked behind her trolley full of cleaning paraphernalia. They reached the door of the penthouse and Jimmy unlocked it. Like the rest of the hotel, the penthouse suite was decorated in shades of grey with the occasional touch of purple. The huge bed was covered with faux fur throws and velvet cushions. Various stone and metal sculptures were placed strategically on the tables and shelves. Shadow picked up a few to test their weight. They were even heavier than they looked. The place was spotlessly clean except for the dark red stain on the deep pale carpet next to a low marble coffee table. The floor-to-ceiling window filled the room with light and gave a view out over the Ouse. Jimmy went to take a look.

"Hey, Chief, you can see your office window from here."

Shadow went to join him and pointed to where his sergeant was looking.

"Yes," he agreed, "and I think those windows down on the left belong to the shop area of La Dolce Vita and that old wooden arched door must be the one we could see in the basement."

Jimmy squinted as he tried to count the windows of the buildings next to the Guildhall. Meanwhile Shadow had tilted his head to one side.

"You can see the place where Jake was sitting when he spotted Anna in the river too," he said.

"Do you think that's important?" asked Jimmy.

"Maybe," replied Shadow, almost to himself.

At that moment, there was a soft knock at the door. Jimmy went over to open it. The maid who had been watching them earlier smiled nervously at him.

"You are police?" she asked in broken English.

"Yes," replied Jimmy.

"Let her in," said Shadow. Jimmy moved aside and the maid stepped cautiously through the door.

"Anna is dead?"

"Yes, she is. I'm sorry. Was she a friend of yours?" asked Shadow.

The maid shook her head. "No, but sometimes we worked the same shifts and she would always smile and say hello. Such a pretty girl."

"Is there something you wanted to tell us, er, Mrs...?"

"Santos. My name is Mia Santos. It is about the towels."

"The towels?" repeated Shadow.

Mia looked exasperated, as if she couldn't find the words she needed. Instead, she went over to the door that led into the bathroom and beckoned for Shadow to follow her. Like the bedroom and sitting area, it was clean and tidy.

"Mr Smith was found here. I heard Anna shout out," said Mia, surprising Shadow by suddenly lying down on the floor herself. "It looked like he fell and banged his head on toilet, you see?" she asked as she demonstrated what she meant by twisting her head at an awkward angle and stretching out her arms.

"Yes, I understand," replied Shadow, offering her his hand to help her back to her feet.

"He had on a robe and his hair was wet, but the towels had not been used," she said, pointing to a stack of three towels in various sizes on the bathroom counter.

"They were dry?" queried Shadow.

"They had not been used. We fold them like this, like how you say the thing you put letter in?"

"Envelope?" suggested Jimmy.

"Yes," said Mia, looking pleased. "They were like this when I came to clean the room. I put out new ones, of course, but I didn't need to. You see?"

She picked up the towel on top of the stack and showed how the corners were folded inward to give a neat square shape. To Shadow it appeared unnecessarily complicated, but he agreed that it was very unlikely the accountant had gone to the trouble of refolding them in that exact way after drying himself.

"You see?" repeated Mia.

"Yes, I do. Thank you very much, Mrs Santos," said Shadow.

Mia looked relieved. "Good. I go now."

She headed quickly to the door, which Jimmy sprang to open for her. When he closed it again, he turned to Shadow.

"It looks like Sophie was right. Smith didn't fall after having a shower. Do you think someone hit him on the head?"

Shadow nodded. "Yes. I guess he was wearing his robe when whoever it was came in and hit him, then moved him to the bathroom, dampened his hair, maybe even put water on the floor, so everyone would think he'd slipped."

"But who? They would have needed to go through reception to find out what room he was in."

Shadow shook his head as he continued to look around the room.

"It must have been someone he knew, if he was happy to let them in, especially if he was wearing only a bathrobe."

"A woman maybe?" suggested Jimmy, then frowned. "But then I guess we shouldn't make assumptions about his private life." He paused, then suddenly looked animated. "Hey, I've had an idea. What if it was Anna who hit him on the head? You heard the night manager – everyone tried it on with her. Suppose Smith made a pass at her and she hit him in self-defence. That could be what was worrying her and why she wanted to talk to you."

Shadow considered the idea for a second, then slowly shook his head.

"From everything we've heard, Anna doesn't sound like the type to lie about something like this. And it doesn't explain who killed her. It's a shame we couldn't get Ben and Ollie over here before they cleaned the place," he grumbled, then seeing Jimmy's crestfallen face said, "Why don't you get on to your new friends over in Leeds? See if anyone there knows about this David Smith character. I don't buy the story about him being a simple accountant giving away free consultations."

"Okay, Chief, but Tom did check already, and he doesn't have any previous convictions."

Shadow began pacing around the room. "Maybe not, but something doesn't feel right. I still don't understand why he would need to stay overnight when Leeds is only an hour away."

"Perhaps he had more than one client to see here."

"Perhaps, but don't you think this place feels a bit flash for a self-employed accountant? Anything he charged his clients would have been eaten up staying here, and according to Ingham, he wasn't even charging them."

"He could just like his creature comforts. Even though he was an accountant, doesn't mean he didn't like flash places. Staying here could have been an early Christmas present to himself."

"If he was that sort of person then you would expect him to have a mobile or a laptop. Where are they?" argued Shadow. "Get in touch with the phone companies; see if they have anything registered in his name."

CHAPTER SIX

Down 2 (7 letters)
We celebrate our union with dinner, dancing and gin

THE TWO OF them left the penthouse suite and were about to return to the lift when Shadow noticed a door marked "fire exit".

"Let's see what's through here," he said, pushing open the heavy door. It led to a small square lobby and then another door opened straight on to the metal fire escape that zigzagged down the full height of the building. Shadow took the hotel room key from Jimmy's hand.

"Go down and see where it leads to, Sergeant. I'll return this to reception and then ask Mr Philips a few more questions."

"But we're five floors up, Chief," protested Jimmy, who had already started shivering as the snowflakes began to settle on his dark hair.

"Then you'd better get a move on. I'll see you at the bottom," replied Shadow briskly. After winding his scarf tightly around his neck, Jimmy began to carefully clunk his way down the metal steps, while Shadow took the lift down to the ground floor. The receptionist looked less than pleased to see him again.

"You mentioned the room had been cleaned," he said as he returned the penthouse key.

"That's right. It's company policy to carry out a deep clean when incidents of this nature occur. Unfortunately, the wine stain could not be removed, so the carpet will need to be replaced before we can book guests in there again."

"Was Mr Smith a regular visitor?"

"No, it was the first time he had stayed with us."

"Did he receive any visitors while he was here?"

"No, at least none that came through reception. I did mention this to one of your colleagues who called earlier," she replied briskly as more guests began to form a queue behind Shadow. He ignored her and pressed on.

"Did he make or receive any phone calls?"

The young woman turned to her computer screen and began tapping at the keyboard. "He made two calls at around seven in the evening."

She scribbled down the numbers and handed them over. One was clearly a mobile number and the other was a Leeds number.

"When did he book the room?" asked Shadow.

This time she didn't need to consult her screen. "He didn't book. He arrived on Thursday afternoon and asked if we had a room available. I dealt with him myself. I told him only the penthouse was available, and he took it."

"Have you got his credit card details?"

She looked a little uncomfortable. "He didn't use a credit card. He paid for the room in advance, in cash."

"Isn't that a little unusual? Don't you usually take details of a card, for security? In case there's any damage to the room, like a badly stained carpet for example."

The young woman flushed red and scowled.

"When I mentioned that was company policy, he left a two-hundred-pound cash deposit."

"Will that cover the cleaning and carpet?"

"No, it won't."

Shadow left her and went in search of Philips, the night manager. He found him still in his office drinking strong black coffee.

"Is it possible to look at the CCTV tapes from Thursday night?"

Philips shook his head. "The tapes are wiped every forty-eight hours. We weren't to know you lot were going to want to see them. Nobody asked us to keep them."

"Very well, and you are sure Mr Smith didn't receive any visitors?"

He looked down. "If you want the truth, I can't be a hundred per cent sure. I was meant to be on reception, but I'd gone into the back office for a quick kip. I'd been there about twenty minutes when Anna came and woke me up to tell me one of the guests had pegged it."

"And you don't recall seeing anyone behaving strangely

after the body was found?"

"No, not in the hotel." He paused. "There was this one guy as I was leaving in the morning. I always go out the rear door and walk home along the river; a lot of the staff do. There was a youngish guy, with an Eastern European accent. He looked like he was waiting for someone. He said 'morning' and said it sounded like we'd had a busy night. I laughed and said that was an understatement. At the time, I wondered if he might be Anna's boyfriend."

"What did he look like?"

"He was about six foot, biggish build, but I couldn't really see his face. He had the zip of his coat pulled right up and a black beanie hat pulled down over his head."

Shadow thanked him and then left the night manager to his coffee and followed the corridor from his office down to the exit. He stepped outside and found Jimmy stamping his feet and shivering as he waited in a small, tarmacked area enclosed by a low stone wall. He pointed to a sign on the wall reading "Assembly Point".

"The fire escape ends around the corner, Chief, and there's an arrow pointing this way," he said through chattering teeth. Shadow gestured to the door behind him.

"That's the way most of the staff leave. The night manager said there was a young Eastern European man waiting here on the morning after Smith died. He thought he might be Anna's boyfriend." Shadow glanced around him – they were only a few feet from the riverside path – then turning back to Jimmy he said, "Come on, let's get back to the office. You're starting to turn blue."

As they crossed Lendal Bridge, Shadow filled Jimmy in on everything else he'd learnt from the receptionist and night manager. He handed him the piece of paper with the two phone numbers Smith had called over.

"See if Tom can find out who these belong to."

They turned on to Lendal and passed by Mr Patel's chemist, and Shadow suddenly remembered their conversation from the previous night.

"By the way, what happened to the three people from the coach park who were taken to the hospital? Had they overdosed?"

"They've all been discharged. It seems they took what they thought was cocaine, but it had been cut with something. Two of them have gone straight back to prison, for breaking the terms of their release. The other was our old friend Kayleigh, but none of them are saying anything about who supplied them. Why do you ask, Chief?"

"I've spoken to Mr Patel. There's no way he missed a delivery."

Jimmy looked at him with interest.

"So we know the boric acid isn't his."

"Yes, but more importantly, we know Joseph lied to us. He lied very quickly and very smoothly when he saw we'd noticed it. He's also been handing out free cups of coffee to the homeless."

"He must have used that as a cover for dealing drugs. Give away a few free samples to get them hooked. It's a classic technique," replied Jimmy immediately. "And remember all the boxes of coffee they had there in the basement. Everyone knows coke's hidden in coffee to put the sniffer dogs off," he continued, warming to his theme. "I bet Anna found out what they were doing, and they killed her to keep her quiet."

Shadow frowned. "I'm not saying you are wrong, but can you really see either Ingham or Woodhouse killing a pretty young woman? I'm not sure I can. Let's pay them another visit and see what they have to say about her."

They stepped under the metal arch that led to the cobbled path that was now slippery with slushy snow. This time La Dolce Vita was open. Dean was now singing "Let It Snow" and Toby was desperately trying to flirt with an attractive blonde who was looking at the many bottles of olive oil. He looked less than pleased to be interrupted by the two detectives.

"We wanted to speak to you about your cleaner, Mr Woodhouse?" explained Shadow.

"Anna? I'm not sure she is our cleaner anymore. She hasn't turned up since Friday and she isn't answering her phone," complained the young man.

"How was she on Friday?"

Toby shrugged. "Okay, a bit quiet, a bit moody."

Shadow and Jimmy exchanged a glance. This was the

first time anyone had said anything less than complimentary about Anna.

"Did she say if anything was wrong? Had something upset her?"

"No, but then she talked to Joe more than me and he wasn't here. He was too busy dishing out coffee to the tramps and beggars."

"You don't agree with him giving away drinks to the homeless?" asked Jimmy.

Toby shrugged. "He says it's good PR. He's started to give it away to crusty students too. I can't see the point myself. If they can't afford a cup of coffee, they are hardly going to be able to shell out twelve quid on a bottle of olive oil. They are more interested in cheap cider than Salice Salentino. More Benson and Hedges than balsamic vinegar."

"Weren't you worried when Anna didn't show up on Monday?" asked Shadow before the young man could come up with any other unnecessary examples to illustrate his point.

"I was more annoyed than worried. The place was a real mess after the weekend. I assumed she'd got a better offer, found someone willing to pay more, but she could have given us some notice. Why are you interested anyway? I thought it was the wine you were bothered about?"

"Is your partner here?"

"No, he's off playing at being Father Christmas again."

"Can I ask where you were on Sunday evening?" continued Shadow. Toby scowled as the young woman gave an apologetic wave and left without making a purchase.

"You chaps aren't exactly good for business, you know! Joe and I were both over on the Dales, at my parents' house near Leyburn. It was my father's sixtieth birthday party. We stayed the night and came back to York in the morning."

"Thank you, Mr Woodhouse," replied Shadow politely. "Now may we take another look at your basement?"

THE TWO DETECTIVES hardly recognised the place when they arrived at the bottom of the steep stairs. It had been thoroughly cleaned since their last visit. Shadow assumed this was down to Joe, who seemed to do most of the hard work. There was now no sign of either the boric acid or the cheap supermarket wine.

"Maybe Joe is trying to push drugs on to students now, Chief," hissed Jimmy when he was sure Toby hadn't followed them.

"Maybe," replied Shadow, "but we still don't have any evidence, except for a glimpse of some boric acid that neither of us bothered to record."

He nodded towards the old wooden door.

"Let's take a look behind there. Check it really does lead down to the river."

Jimmy slid the bolt back with ease and a cold gust of

wind hit them in the face as the door swung open. The two detectives peered into the old brick tunnel behind. It sloped gently downwards and it was possible to hear the low roar and splash of the river.

"How long do you think it is?" asked Jimmy.

"About thirty or forty feet," suggested Shadow, kneeling down to take a closer look at the tunnel floor.

"What's that? About ten metres?" queried Jimmy, checking the calculator on his phone. "Do you think this basement ever floods?"

"No, I think the tunnel is too long, but it is a good way of quietly bringing goods in or disposing of them."

"Like drugs or a body, you mean? Do you think this is how Anna ended up in the river?"

"It would make sense. It's close to where she was found, but Ingham and Woodhouse both sound like they have an alibi for Sunday night."

"Should we try to get forensics to take a look?"

"We'd need a warrant. To give them credit, Ingham and Woodhouse haven't objected to us looking around, but bringing Ben and Ollie in might be a different story. Besides, the water level will have dropped since Sunday," said Shadow, who was more aware than most of the state of the river. "The chances are if there something here it's been washed away. And another thing, she was dressed up, as if she was going out for the evening. Would she really have been wearing a black dress and high heels to come to the place where she works as a cleaner?"

Shadow stepped back from the tunnel, deep in thought as he considered what might have brought Anna to the basement on a Sunday evening. Jimmy carefully closed the tunnel door as his phone pinged. He looked at the screen.

"It's a text from Tom, Chief. He's traced the two calls Smith made from the hotel. One was to a public call box in Leeds and the other was to here, La Dolce Vita."

"Are you two going to be much longer? I want to close soon. I've got a hot date tonight," called out Toby as he came heavily down the stairs. Shadow thought this was more likely wishful thinking on the young man's part.

"Did Mr Smith telephone here on Thursday at about seven o'clock?"

Toby shrugged. "He might have done. Joe would probably have taken it. It's late-night opening on Thursdays. I was up in the shop until eight."

Shadow pointed to the far corner of the basement.

"Are you able to open the safe for us, Mr Woodhouse?"

Toby shook his head.

"No can do, Chief Inspector. Only Joe knows the combination. He keeps changing it. He says it's for security reasons, but it got me into hot water when I couldn't get to the rent the other day."

"You pay your rent in cash?" asked Jimmy, "Isn't that a bit unusual?" Toby flushed in embarrassment.

"The owner of the property insisted. There were a couple

of glitches with our direct debit, then a cheque bounced. I tried to explain, but they were adamant. It's cash only from now on."

"Don't you have a very understanding landlord?"

"You have no idea, Chief Inspector," replied Toby with a wry smile as he opened the door into the courtyard wide and not very subtly said, "Have a good evening, gents. I won't keep you any longer."

The two detectives stepped out into the courtyard and Toby closed the door behind them with a heavy bang.

"Do you think it was weird that Woodhouse didn't want to know why we were asking about Anna?" asked Jimmy as he trudged over the snow-speckled cobbles. "Maybe he didn't need to ask because he knows what happened to her."

"Or maybe he didn't care. Now she isn't cleaning for them, she's of no interest to him. He does seem a little self-absorbed, and although he doesn't come across as being very clever, surely if you'd killed someone, you'd feign innocence when talking to the police."

"I guess you're right, Chief," Jimmy said with a sigh.

BACK AT THE station, Shadow checked which officers were on duty that night. He requested they pay a visit to La Maison du Fleuve and speak with the night shift staff. In particular, he wanted them check if anyone else had seen or spoken to the man Philips had described. He was about to return to his office when Jimmy thrust his mobile phone in front of Shadow's face.

"Look what I found, Chief," he said. Shadow put on his glasses, but he still struggled to make out the image on the tiny screen.

"What am I meant to be looking at exactly, Sergeant?" he enquired.

"I thought I'd check out Toby's story about being at his father's birthday party, so I had a look on his Facebook page and he and Joe were definitely there and so was someone else we know. Look, it's Sir Charles Richmond. I'll enlarge it for you."

Shadow squinted and sure enough there was Sir Charles, a local member of parliament, holding a glass of champagne and smiling a little awkwardly next to Toby, who was grinning broadly and had his arm around the shoulder of the older man. Sir Charles had been very helpful during an investigation earlier in the year and Shadow valued his opinion.

"Good work, Sergeant. I'll call Sir Charles and see if he can confirm Woodhouse and Ingham were there all night. In the meantime, you check if either of them has a criminal record."

Shadow phoned the MP's office and a little over an hour later Sir Charles called him back.

"Yes, I was at Jumbo Woodhouse's birthday party on

Sunday, Chief Inspector. He has one of the largest estates in my constituency. I've known the family for years," he replied when Shadow explained what his enquiry was about.

"Can you remember seeing Toby Woodhouse and his friend Joseph Ingham?"

"Toby certainly. He's Jumbo's youngest son, a cheerful enough young man, but he doesn't seem to stick at anything. I think his family are hoping he might make something of himself with this latest venture. And yes, I was introduced to his business partner. A tall, earnest-looking chap. Apparently they are old school friends."

"Neither of them left early?"

"No, Chief Inspector. Jumbo didn't start his speech until midnight and by one o'clock he was only up to his university days." Sir Charles laughed. "I left at about two thirty, but plenty were still there dancing, including Toby and his friend. Both had been drinking. I certainly don't think either of them would have been capable of driving. Why, has something happened?"

"Yes," admitted Shadow cautiously, "there's a chance Toby might be involved in a case we are investigating."

"Oh dear," replied Sir Charles. "Jumbo won't be happy."

Shadow replaced the receiver as Jimmy appeared in the open doorway brandishing his electronic notebook.

"I've checked up on Ingham and Woodhouse, Chief. I couldn't find a home address for either of them, but I asked around and apparently Toby's dad has a boat moored at

Naburn that they have been staying on – a bit like you, Chief – and they sometimes crash in the shop basement, which might explain the mess. Toby's been banned from driving for twelve months for speeding and Joe's had a caution a few years ago for possession, so there's a link to drugs."

Shadow raised an eyebrow. "It's a bit tenuous, Sergeant. How many students caught with a joint go on to deal cocaine? But it might explain why Toby had to sit the licensing exams," he replied as he glanced at his watch, then rose to his feet and reached for his jacket. "Anything else?"

"No, Chief. I'm still waiting for Inspector Grabowski to return my call about David Smith. Are you leaving?"

"Yes, Luisa's brother should be at his hotel by now. While I'm away try to track down Jake. See if Anna ever mentioned Toby or Joe to him."

"Will do, Chief. Good luck!"

"Thanks," muttered Shadow, hoping he wouldn't need it.

A FEW MOMENTS later, Shadow found himself in the reception of the Dean Court Hotel waiting for Luca to come down and meet him. He couldn't remember when he had last felt this nervous. They had met briefly, when Luisa's brother was only sixteen. He had come over to London with his parents to take his sister's body back to Italy. Drowning in his own grief, Shadow could only vaguely remember a tall, angular young man who looked shell-shocked and was doing his best to support his distraught mother.

Shadow paced up and down on the polished wooden floor, trying not to get in the way of other guests. Classical music was playing softly in the background. He stopped abruptly at the ping of the lift's bell. Despite the years, Shadow recognised Luca instantly as he stepped through the sliding doors and came striding across the foyer. Immaculately dressed in a navy suit and white shirt with a deep mahogany tan, he had a broad smile that immediately reminded Shadow of Luisa. Shadow stepped forward and stiffly held out his hand, but the Italian brushed it aside and instead enveloped him in a huge hug.

"John, how good it is to see you again," he cried.

"Hello, Luca," Shadow replied, awkwardly patting the younger man on the back. Luca stepped back, but his hands remained on Shadow's shoulders as he began to shake his head.

"It has been so long. Over twenty-six years since we lost our beautiful Luisa. One of my deepest regrets is that my family did not remain in contact with you."

Shadow attempted a shrug. "It's understandable. I know your parents partly held me responsible for what happened. If Luisa had returned to Italy as they wanted her to…" he paused "…but I asked her to stay, and…"

Luca removed his hands from Shadow's shoulders and held them up to silence him.

"No, no, you must not think that way. My parents were upset. They spoke without thinking. Luisa always did as she wanted. You mustn't blame yourself. She stayed with you because she loved you."

Shadow shifted uncomfortably. Other hotel guests were beginning to stop and stare, and he could feel his throat begin to tighten. The years seemed to have melted away and losing Luisa suddenly felt very raw again. He gave a small cough and attempted a smile.

"Let's go and get something to eat," he suggested. "You must be starving after your trip."

Shadow had booked the two of them a table at Catania's. Gino and Maria had never met Luca before, but they had bought wine from his family for years and greeted him like a long-lost friend. When Maria finally stopped hugging him, they took their seats at a corner table and both ordered the *gamberoni* followed by the *medaglioni di manzo*. Gino brought them a bottle of Luca's wine and poured out two glasses. Luca cleared his throat and raised his glass.

"What should we drink to, John?" he asked.

"The past?" suggested Shadow, raising his own glass.

Luca inclined his head. "And the future," he added. "*Salute*, my friend."

"*Alla nostra salute*," replied Shadow, taking a sip of wine. He reached down into the bag he'd brought with him, removed the bottle of Greco Salice Salentino he'd retrieved from Neville and placed it on the table.

"We found traces of peanut oil in the bottle of wine the dean drank from when she became ill. This bottle was also bought from La Dolce Vita. I'd like you to taste it as I suspect it may not be genuine," he explained.

"Certainly," replied Luca as he studied the bottle, "but I can tell you now, that is not my wine."

"How can you be so sure?" asked Shadow, putting on his reading glasses and peering more closely.

"The label is wrong. It's a good copy, but it is not my label and the glass the bottle is made of, it is too thin."

Shadow picked up the bottle, comparing it to the one they were drinking from. Luca was right. The label on Neville's bottle was more faded and on thinner paper and the glass the bottle was made from was a paler shade of green and felt lighter in weight. He beckoned Gino back over and asked him for a bottle opener and two extra glasses. Then he poured out a small amount of Neville's wine into each glass. Luca took a sniff and pulled a face before both men took a sip. They both grimaced in disgust at the sharp, sour liquid.

"As they say in your courtrooms, I rest my case," said Luca, taking a large swig of his genuine wine to remove the bitter aftertaste. "I doubt the grapes used to make that wine have ever been anywhere near Italy. It tastes like a merlot perhaps from Spain or some New World place," he continued with a slight sneer of disdain. Then he looked at Shadow with anger in his eyes. "John, you must help me do something about the people who are selling this filth under my name. They will ruin my business."

"That won't happen. We'll deal with them tomorrow. Trading standards are already looking into the case. They'll be able to seize and destroy the fake wine."

Luca took another sip of his wine and appeared to be pacified by this news. Shadow smiled to himself. Luca was so like Luisa. She had been the same. Firing up at the first sign of any injustice but calming down just as quickly. He was now fiddling with his mobile phone.

"Excuse me, John. I am not being rude, but I promised my wife and children I would introduce you to them as soon as I could."

He turned the screen towards Shadow, who was immediately greeted with loud, heavily accented cries of "Hello, John." Shadow adjusted his glasses and peered at the screen. Smiling and waving at him were a very attractive dark-haired woman surrounded by two teenagers and two younger children. He raised his hand in greeting.

"Hello," he replied tentatively.

"John, this is my wife, Bianca. My sons, Antonio and Matteo, and my daughters, Luisa and little Caterina."

"Luisa?" queried Shadow immediately.

"Named after her beautiful aunt," explained Luca. Shadow peered more closely at the teenage girl, standing shyly behind her mother.

"It is nice to meet you, John," said Bianca.

"They all know who I am?" Shadow asked in surprise.

"But of course. There are many photos of you and Luisa in our home. Luisa was always sending pictures home with her letters. The children love to hear about how she lived on a boat in London."

"You look like your pictures," said Bianca politely. "We hope you will come and see us one day."

"Thank you very much. That's very kind," replied Shadow.

"Do you still live on a boat?" asked Luisa, ignoring her siblings as they giggled at her speaking English.

"Yes, I do, Luisa," replied Shadow with a smile.

"Now we must go before our food arrives," declared Luca. "Say goodbye now." There was a chorus of goodbyes as Shadow raised his hand and Luca blew kisses to his family before turning off the phone.

"Bianca means it. She made me promise I would invite you to spend Christmas with us and do you really still live on a boat? The same boat? *Florence*, yes?"

"Yes," replied Shadow. "I left London and brought her north."

"I would like to see her very much. See where Luisa was so happy."

"Of course," agreed Shadow as Gino brought their food to the table.

IT WAS LATE when Shadow finally left Catania's. The air was cold and crisp as he walked through the silent streets back to *Florence.* He had left Luca behind still chatting to Gino and Maria. The more the wine flowed, the more his companions had lapsed into Italian, and Shadow was too exhausted to try to keep up with the conversation. It had been a long, tiring day, but when he lay down and closed his eyes, sleep eluded him. Seeing Luca, after all these years, was unsettling.

Once Shadow had assured him that they would get to the bottom of where the fake wine was coming from, they had spent hours discussing his family and reminiscing. Both his parents had passed away and were buried close to their daughter, and Luca admitted neither of them had ever recovered from losing her, but that the arrival of grandchildren had helped ease their pain. He explained that he'd promised he would do everything he could to keep his sister's memory alive and Shadow, who for years could barely bring himself to speak her name, had been quite overwhelmed to hear Luca's young family knew so much about the aunt they would never meet.

CHAPTER SEVEN

Across 9 (7 letters)
Keep your pet and rice as proof of purchase

THE NEXT MORNING, Shadow had arranged to meet Luca at Bettys for breakfast. It felt strange to have someone sitting opposite him when usually his only companion was the *Yorkshire Post* crossword. As always Shadow ordered a pot of tea and a full English. He tried not to look disappointed when his companion only chose a coffee and croissant.

"Are you sure that's all you want?" he queried.

"I'm never very hungry in the morning," replied Luca slightly apologetically, wincing as he removed his sunglasses. "And perhaps I overindulged a little last night too."

Shadow nodded, then in the mirror he suddenly caught sight of the glamorous dark-haired woman he'd seen at La Dolce Vita. She was gliding towards a window table and shuffling along in her wake was the elderly gentleman in the black hat he'd also seen leaving the wine shop. Shadow turned to watch them. Luca followed his gaze, then gasped and quickly looked away.

"What's wrong?" asked Shadow. "Do you know her?"

"Not her, him. The man you were watching – don't you know who he is?" Luca hissed.

Shadow shook his head.

"It's Don Rossetti," continued Luca. "Back home, he's the head of the Sacra Corona Unita."

"The Mafia? Are you sure?" asked Shadow incredulously as he strained his neck to get a better view of the old man, who had finally removed his hat.

"It's what we call the Mafia and trust me, John, you don't live in Lecce and not know who Don Rossetti is," Luca hissed.

"What on earth is he doing in North Yorkshire?" asked Shadow.

"I heard," began Luca, then paused as the waitress placed the tea and coffee on the table. "I heard," he continued in hushed tones when she'd gone, "that he'd been forced into hiding. For many years, he ruled our area with an iron fist, but as he grew older, his health began to suffer. With no son to follow him, his two nephews began arguing about who would take control when he'd gone. Then a violent power struggle between the two sides broke out. As Don Rossetti grew weaker, he became vulnerable. A rumour went round that he had fled Italy for his own safety. It seems that rumour is true."

"And the lady he's with, is that his wife, his daughter?"

Luca raised his cup to his lips and attempted to look

across the room discreetly. "I don't know. I've never seen her before." He paused and wrinkled his forehead. "I believe he was married with a daughter, but thirty, maybe forty years ago they disappeared. It was at a time when Italy was plagued by kidnappers taking the children of prominent or wealthy individuals. The feeling amongst the people of Lecce was that they had been hidden for their own safety. I certainly never remember seeing them, but my mother mentioned them once or twice I think."

At that moment, their breakfast arrived, and the two men were briefly distracted, but Shadow couldn't stop wondering what had brought an elderly Mafioso to York. It seemed that the presence of Don Rossetti was also on Luca's mind, as he barely touched his croissant. When they'd finished and stood up to leave, Shadow felt the eyes of the dark-haired woman on them. He turned and nodded politely at her, but only received an imperious look in return.

AFTER BREAKFAST, AT Luca's insistence, they headed straight to La Dolce Vita. Shadow would have preferred to discuss the matter with the council's trading standards officers first, but Luca was adamant that he wanted to meet the two young men who were damaging his reputation as soon as possible. As they made their way across St Helen's Square, Jimmy appeared from the station to join them.

"How are you enjoying York, Mr Greco?" asked Jimmy politely after Shadow had introduced them.

"It is a beautiful city, but very cold," replied Luca, who like the sergeant was half hidden by a huge scarf. "At home it is still fourteen or fifteen degrees even now. It is more pleasant, I think. I have invited John to come over and join us for Christmas."

Jimmy grinned at Shadow. "You should go, Chief. You'd love it. Think of all the food and wine." Then turning to Luca: "He never goes on holiday. He must have built up loads of leave."

"Then we must both try to convince him, Sergeant," replied Luca as the three of them made their way down the cobbled path to La Dolce Vita. However, they arrived to find the shop in darkness. Jimmy knocked loudly on the door, but there was no response. Shadow checked the opening times written on a sign in the window.

"They should be open by now," he said.

"Those two open on time? That'll be the day," said a voice from above them. They looked up to find Bob, the window cleaner, at the top of his ladder.

"Can't we break down the door?" demanded Luca impatiently.

"Not without a warrant," replied Shadow, "and that might take a while." He turned to Jimmy. "See if you can find out who owns the building, but first get on to trading standards. Tell them we have Luca with us and that he's confirmed the wine Neville bought here isn't Greco Salice Salentino."

Jimmy nodded and dialled the number on his phone. He spoke to the trading standards officer, then covered the mouthpiece and addressed Luca. "He wants to know if you are prepared to make a statement?"

"Absolutely!" declared Luca. "I will go there immediately. There is a taxi rank outside the hotel."

Jimmy scribbled down the name and the address for the trading standards officer as he continued to talk to him on the phone and handed it over to Luca.

"Do you want me to come with you?" offered Shadow, but Luca shook his head.

"No, you have a murder to investigate. I will come and find you when I have made my statement."

With that he took the piece of paper and strode purposefully away.

"I can tell you who owns the building," said Bob, who had been watching the proceedings intently and was now climbing down his ladder. "It's the Black Widow."

Shadow put out his hand to steady the ladder that was wobbling precariously on the loose cobbles.

"Who's that?" he asked as Jimmy finished his phone call.

"Her real name is Barbara Smith. You must have seen her about. She looks like she belongs in New York, not this York. Long black hair, full-length fur coats. You can't miss her. She owns loads of property in Leeds as well as here, and she's been married at least three times. When this place was empty, she used to pay me to do the windows. Always gave a decent tip."

Shadow nodded, sure Bob had described the woman he'd just seen in Bettys.

"Thanks, Bob. By the way, do you ever remember seeing a young blonde woman here on weekday mornings?"

Bob's face broke into a smile. "Do you mean Anna? She's a lovely girl. Now she did get here early. She'd let herself in through there," he said, pointing to the door into the basement. "She'd always offer to make me a cuppa if she saw me. Has something happened to her?"

"Yes, I'm afraid we think she's dead. We found a body in the river, it's almost definitely her," replied Shadow.

Bob's face fell. He shook his head and picked up his ladder and bucket. "Poor girl! It's always the good ones. If you find those two chancers, let me know. They owe me for three weeks," he called over his shoulder as he headed up the cobbled path.

"At least that solves the mystery of the other key Anna had," said Jimmy, who had removed the evidence bag containing Anna's keys from his pocket and was trying the third key in the lock. "Bingo, Chief! Do you want to go inside?"

Shadow shook his head.

"No, we're not going to risk the investigation by carrying out an illegal search," he said as he continued to think.

"Besides Bob told us something even more important. We now know the identity of Ingham and Woodhouse's landlord or rather landlady. I'm almost certain Barbara Smith is the dark-haired lady who was arriving as we were leaving yesterday. In which case, things may have become a lot more complicated."

"Why's that, Chief?"

Shadow briefly recounted his visit to Bettys that morning and Luca's reaction to their two fellow diners. Jimmy stared at him open-mouthed.

"Seriously? Don Rossetti is here in York?"

"Luca seemed convinced. Why, have you heard of him?"

"Of course I have; he's notorious. Only the other week I was watching a documentary about the Sacra Corona Unita. They said he'd been in charge of the area around Lecce for years. I can't believe he was that little old guy!"

"Appearances can be deceiving," replied Shadow. "It doesn't look like Ingham or Woodhouse are arriving any time soon. Let's get back to the office."

"You don't think Barbara Smith and David Smith could be connected, do you, Chief?" asked Jimmy as they made their way back up the path to the station. "Billy said she'd been married a lot."

"It's worth checking, but it's a very common name. Anything else to report?" asked Shadow as they edged past a large Christmas tree two uniformed constables were trying to manoeuvre into position in the reception area.

"Yes, Chief. I went to the Salvation Army first thing to speak to Jake. He said Anna had occasionally mentioned meeting a boyfriend but didn't give any details. He didn't know the name of the place Anna worked as a cleaner, but she'd complained about one of the guys who worked there always trying to chat her up. The description she gave, chubby and blond, sounded like Toby Woodhouse. I was thinking maybe he got angry when she kept rebuffing him."

Shadow nodded thoughtfully. "But he has an alibi for Sunday. Did Jake say anything else?"

"No, he wasn't really in the mood to talk. I don't think he's very happy with us?"

"Why?"

Jimmy shifted uncomfortably from foot to foot. "It's because of the *Herald*. The first report of a body being removed from the river was accompanied by the photograph of you and me and Jake walking towards your boat and it said a local man was helping us with our inquiries. Well, apparently a few people recognised Jake and Missy. They put two and two together and got five. They thought he must be involved somehow. He's had quite a bit of abuse and has had to find somewhere else to sleep. He's left his usual spot under Lendal Bridge."

Shadow picked up the copy of the *Herald* that was lying on the reception desk. The photo was blurred, but Jimmy was right: anyone who knew Jake and Missy would probably be able to identify them.

"What's MacNab playing at? Printing this without any explanation."

Jimmy shrugged. "I guess he thought it might be a scoop and, let's face it, Jake isn't really in a position to take legal action, is he?"

Shadow grunted as he continued to read. "Why isn't there any mention of Anna by name or her picture? We'll never get any response from the public."

Jimmy and Tom, who was standing behind the desk, exchanged an awkward glance.

"We couldn't release her name, Chief," explained Jimmy. "Her parents haven't been informed yet."

"Why not? Couldn't the Slovenian police find them?"

"It's my fault, Chief," admitted Tom, flushing bright red. "I misheard Jimmy. I thought he said Slovakian police. By the time I realised my mistake, it was too late to call them yesterday. I'm really sorry."

"For crying out loud, you are as bad as that useless manager from the hotel. I hope you've asked Father Christmas for an atlas," fumed Shadow. "We can't wait any longer to formally identify her. You'll have to arrange for Francesco to do it and make sure you accompany him." Then turning to Jimmy: "Release a press statement saying nobody is currently helping us with our inquiries and we are very grateful to a member of the public who spotted the body and alerted us."

"Shouldn't we let the press office at HQ deal with it from now on?" asked Jimmy.

"No, it's our mess. We'll clear it up," he snapped. "And tell MacNab if that picture of Jake appears again, I'll sue him myself."

Despairing at both the journalist and his young colleague, Shadow headed to his office and began routing through his desk drawers for indigestion tablets. He had only been at his desk a moment when his phone began to ring. It was Ben from forensics.

"Morning, Chief. How's everything with you?" he said cheerfully, but Shadow was in no mood to chat.

"What do you have to tell me about the stone and rope that were tied to Anna?"

"Technically, it's not a stone, it's been smoothed over and there are remnants of concrete stuck on it. I'd say it's more of a cobble and, having spoken to Sophie, we think it could have been used to hit her on the back on the head. It's the right shape, size and weight."

"And the rope?"

"Technically, not really a rope," replied Ben, and Shadow raised his eyes to the ceiling, wishing as he often did when speaking to his forensics team that he had been blessed with patience. "It's made from the same fabric as the dress she was wearing and was plaited. We think it was probably the belt for the dress. By the way, we checked the label and the dress was from an Italian high street fashion chain. Ollie checked with their head office. It was part of their range two years ago. Jimmy said she spoke Italian, so we thought she might have lived there for a while. Italy is next door to Slovenia after all."

"Possibly," pondered Shadow, "but let's get back to the stone and rope. You're telling me she was hit on the head with a cobblestone and then they used her own belt to tie the cobble to her ankle, before pushing her in the river," re-capped Shadow.

"That's it, Chief. Got it in one."

"Is there any way you can tell where the cobble is from?" asked Shadow, his mind wandering back to Bob's ladder balancing on the loose stones down by La Dolce Vita.

"Not really, Chief. It was in the water over twenty-four hours, so any soil or moss or whatever that we could have used would have been washed off."

"Any luck tracing her phone?"

"Jimmy gave us the number you got from Lucia. It was a pay-as-you-go phone. The phone company told us it was last active on Sunday evening. She used it to call another pay-as-you-go number and they could only narrow the location down to within a few hundred metres of where we found her, but we know she was probably killed quite close to the river, so that doesn't really help much, does it, Chief?"

"No, it doesn't," agreed Shadow with a sigh.

No sooner had he put the phone down than there was a knock at the door.

"Yes?" he called out.

"Only me, Chief," said Jimmy as he entered the room

holding a laptop. "I wanted to update you on the officers who went to speak to the night shift workers at the hotel last night. They said Philips was right: most of them do leave through that exit. A few of them recalled seeing the man with the beanie hat when they left on Friday morning, but nobody spoke to him. It sounds like they were all too distracted by one of their guests dying."

"Anything else?"

"Yes. They also asked about Anna and the last time her colleagues had seen her. One of the other waitresses said that before Anna left on Sunday, at about one am, she changed out of her uniform and into a black dress and heels."

"The clothing we found her wearing?"

"Yes, Chief. The other waitress asked if she had a hot date, but Anna just laughed."

Shadow nodded thoughtfully. "Anything else?"

"I've been googling Don Rossetti," he said, opening up the laptop as he took a seat opposite Shadow.

"And?"

"What Luca told you seems to add up. About forty years ago, there was a spate of high-profile kidnappings in Italy, often involving the wives and children of prominent citizens. It was rumoured Don Rossetti, who had recently taken control of the organisation, sent his wife and young daughter away to keep them safe, but nobody knew where. Imagine going to such extreme lengths to keep them safe. Apparently, he had the two guys who did know where they were killed so they couldn't tell anyone else."

Shadow raised a sceptical eyebrow. "There's a lot of rumour and apparently going on. I don't suppose you've managed to find something useful like a photo of him?"

"Yes, there's a mug shot, but it must be about fifty years old."

Jimmy turned the laptop around and Shadow squinted at the grainy black-and-white image on the screen. It was impossible to tell if it was the elderly man he'd seen having breakfast that morning.

"We need to speak to Barbara Smith as soon as possible and confirm that she is the woman I saw with Don Rossetti and, if she is, how they are connected."

"Actually, Chief, that's why I'm here," interrupted Tom, who had appeared a few seconds earlier and was now hovering in the doorway looking sheepish. "A woman by the name of Barbara Smith came to the reception desk and left a message for you. She said she would be waiting to speak with you in Harkers."

"When?"

"Now, Chief. I said I would pass the message on, but she didn't wait for an answer. I got the impression she expected you to accept the invitation."

"How did she even know I was here?" muttered Shadow, getting to his feet and reaching for his wax jacket.

"I've told you, Chief, the Mafia know everything," said Jimmy, shaking his head. "Do you want me to come with you?"

"She's part of the Mafia?" asked Tom incredulously. "Maybe you shouldn't go alone, Chief."

"Oh, calm down, the pair of you. We don't know for sure if she is related to Don Rossetti or if she's involved in any of his activities and I'm sure if anyone was going to try to bump me off, they would choose a more discreet location than a wine bar in the centre of the city," he said, pulling on his jacket.

He left his two younger colleagues behind at the station and crossed St Helen's Square to the elegant Georgian building that was home to Harkers wine bar. He spotted her immediately. She was sitting at a small marble table on the raised platform by the window, sipping a martini. He raised his hand in greeting and she acknowledged him with a slight inclination of her head. He ordered himself a glass of red wine and went to join her.

"I hear you have been making inquiries about two of my tenants," she said as he sat down opposite her.

"Yes, Mr Ingham and Mr Woodhouse."

"May I ask why?"

"We believe they have been behaving fraudulently. Selling cheap wine under more expensive labels."

"I see."

"Now may I ask you a question, Mrs Smith?"

There was another slight inclination of the head.

"I understand you are a successful businesswoman, with a

large property portfolio. Why would you agree to rent one of your properties to two young men with no experience in business?"

"You are quite correct. In normal circumstances they would not be my tenants of choice. However, the parents of Mr Woodhouse are very wealthy. They paid three months' rent in advance."

"They have been there eight months. Have they paid the last five months on time?" he asked, although he already knew the answer.

"Not always, but they have always paid eventually," she conceded. "I now insist on cash only, although there was a slight delay with their latest payment. It was due on Friday morning, but Toby gave me some excuse about not being able to open the safe. I collected it on Monday instead."

"We called there earlier this morning, but the place was deserted."

"I am not surprised," she replied, taking a sip of her martini. "I don't approve of the way they conduct their business, Chief Inspector. When their lease expires, I have no plans to renew it."

From the corner of his eye, Shadow could see Jimmy lurking on the other side of the street, straining his neck, trying to look through the window.

"That's a shame," he said.

Barbara shrugged and Shadow decided to take a chance.

"Your father seemed to like the place."

Barbara surveyed him through narrowed eyes for a moment before replying, "He liked the coffee they made there. It was the brand he drank at home and the tall thin one could speak very good Italian. They say women gossip but believe me nobody likes to talk more than old men with stories to tell. He also liked the pretty girl, who cleaned for them."

"Anna? Did you know we are investigating her murder?" he asked, although he suspected there was very little that happened in the city that Barbara Smith didn't know about.

"Yes," she replied without a flicker of emotion. "My father was sorry to hear about it. She also spoke Italian. He would time his visits for when she was there. I think he flirted with her a little. I told him he was an old fool. He said he might be old, but he would need to be dead before he stopped appreciating beautiful women."

"Is your mother no longer alive?"

Barbara's jet-black eyes flickered for a second.

"No, she died before she could be reunited with my father."

"It must have been difficult for her alone in a foreign country all those years. Were there any other men in her life?"

Barbara looked at him with something close to pity. "If you think she would ever consider such a thing, then you really don't understand my family at all, Chief Inspector."

Shadow took a sip of his wine, and quickly changed the

subject. "I haven't seen your father in any of the city's Italian restaurants."

Barbara raised a dark, heavily pencilled eyebrow.

"We have decided that is not a good idea. It is better if people at home…well, it is better if they don't know he is here."

"He must be happy to be living here with you."

"No! He thinks it is a cold and damp place. He misses the sun. Now, if you will excuse me, Chief Inspector, I think we have both said and heard everything we needed to."

Shadow stood and watched her leave before downing the last of his wine and following her out.

"You'll never make an undercover officer, Sergeant," he said as a relieved-looking Jimmy came jogging over.

"What did she want?" asked his sergeant eagerly.

"I'll fill you in back at the station," replied Shadow as he headed back across the square.

THEY RETURNED TO the incident room and Shadow shared the information he'd received from Barbara with his colleagues.

"So she as good as admitted Don Rossetti is her father?" said Jimmy. "Then that must be the connection to the drugs. The Sacra Corona Unita controlled the cocaine trade in their area. They must be using La Dolce Vita as a front; that's why

Woodhouse and Ingham aren't bothered about making any money."

Shadow frowned and shook his head. "If that was the case, I don't think they would be permitted to draw attention to themselves by selling fake wine," he argued.

"Which is why Barbara isn't renewing the lease," countered Jimmy.

"What about Anna? I believed Barbara when she said her father was fond of her. Why would they kill her?"

"She'd found out about the drugs, but because she spoke Italian, she also knew who she was dealing with and was scared, which was why she needed to talk to you privately."

Shadow continued shaking his head. "I'm not convinced. And what about David Smith?"

"He'd found out what was going on too."

At that moment, the telephone on the desk rang. Jimmy picked it up. "Luca is down at the front desk, Chief," he said as he replaced the receiver.

"I'll go and see how he got on at trading standards," Shadow said as he rose to his feet. "You keep trying Grabowski. Ask her if there is a chance the Sacra Corona Unita are operating over here; if anyone should know, it's the National Crime Agency."

HE FOUND LUCA chatting to Tom and admiring the

Christmas tree that was now in place.

"How did it go with trading standards?" asked Shadow.

"Excellent," replied Luca with a wide smile. "They were very helpful. They will be visiting La Dolce Vita and seizing the fake wine. They will also tell the newspapers that my wine is good to drink again."

"That is good news," replied Shadow. "And what do you plan to do now?"

"There is a shop here in York that wanted to place quite a large order with me. When you told me what had happened, I was worried they would cancel the order. That is partly why I wanted to come here in person. I would like to pay them a visit and reassure them that everything is okay. It is called Bacchus. It has a strange address, but if you wait a moment, I'll find it," said Luca, beginning to scroll through his phone.

"No need," replied Shadow, heading towards the door. "It's on Shambles. I know it well. I'll take you there myself."

BACCHUS WAS OWNED by Oliver Harrison, a smartly dressed middle-aged man with a neatly trimmed beard and a bow tie. A couple of years before, Shadow had solved the mystery of what had happened to Emma, his missing sister. He smiled broadly when the two men ducked under the low doorway.

"Chief Inspector Shadow! How good to see you," he

said, shaking the detective warmly by the hand. "To what do I owe the pleasure?"

"I'd like to introduce you to a friend of mine, Luca Greco, from the Greco winery."

Oliver was delighted to meet Luca in person, and as the two men immediately began chatting about wine, Shadow glanced around the small, but well-stocked shop. He noticed there were several gift boxes of wine and hampers pre-wrapped for people to buy as Christmas gifts. There was one containing six of his favourite Italian wines and decorated with a large red bow.

"Can I arrange to have this delivered to someone?" he asked a young man who was restocking some shelves.

"Of course, sir. If you can just jot the name and address of the recipient down here, and I'll organise the rest," replied the young man, handing a notepad over. Shadow began writing down Neville Prentis's address, then remembered the hours Marjorie was at work.

"It needs to be delivered in the morning and I'd like it to be anonymous. Is that a problem?"

"Not at all, sir."

Shadow handed over his credit card.

"I won't be a moment, sir," said the young man. "I'm not eighteen until February, so my colleague will have to take payment."

He waved to the older lady, who was making up more gift boxes, and she hurried over with the card machine.

"Isn't it a little difficult to work here when you can't legally sell alcohol?" enquired Shadow when the young man had thanked his colleague and handed him his card and receipt back.

"Oh, I'm only helping out over the Christmas holidays, taking orders and making deliveries – that sort of thing. I'm in the sixth form at St John's and Oliver is an old boy. He put up an advert on the noticeboard outside our common room. He often needs help at this time of year and over the summer when there are loads of tourists here."

Shadow nodded, then a thought occurred to him. "I don't suppose you remember two other St John's old boys, Toby Woodhouse and Joseph Ingham?"

The young man grinned. "Yes, I know Toby and Joe. They were in the same year as my older brother. I saw them last week at the school carol service at the Minster. I was quite surprised to see them back in York."

"They've opened a shop down by Lendal Cellars," explained Shadow, keen to hear what else the young man might have to say.

"Really? Well, they were always hanging around together at school, although I never thought they had much in common. Joe was really clever; he was there on a full scholarship and Toby, well, he's not that bright, but his family are loaded. Joe saw himself as a bit of an entrepreneur. He would go to the cash and carry and buy sweets in bulk and then undercut the tuck shop prices. When he was older, he would buy up tickets for local club nights and sell them on at a much higher price. I can't say it made him very popular."

"You said you were surprised to see them back in York."

"Yes, the last I'd heard, they'd gone travelling round Europe and then Joe had a place to study chemistry down in London, but maybe that fell through."

Shadow nodded and thanked the young man for his help. Luca and Oliver were still deep in conversation about this year's grape harvest, so Shadow arranged to meet him later at his hotel. He left the crowded Shambles thinking about what he'd learnt about Toby and Joseph. As he made his way down Coney Street, he suddenly saw Toby coming towards on him on his bike and recalled Jimmy mentioning he'd lost his driving licence. The young man was wearing a large hat with earflaps and weaving unsteadily through the Christmas shoppers. Shadow held up his hand to stop him.

"You do know you're going the wrong way on a one-way street, don't you, Mr Woodhouse?" he asked.

Toby's bike squealed to a halt. The red-faced young man rolled his eyes as he struggled to catch his breath.

"Seriously? Isn't a traffic offence a bit below the pay grade of a chief inspector? I'm having one hell of a day as it is. I was a bit late opening up, then I got a call from trading standards threatening to close us down, the Black Widow is on the warpath and Joe has gone AWOL. I couldn't take anymore. I'm going home." He gasped before setting off again at a wobbly pace.

Shadow watched him go. If Toby Woodhouse was a criminal mastermind, he was very good at hiding it, and what did he mean by Joe being AWOL? Shadow sincerely hoped it didn't mean they were about to find another body. He returned to the station and picked up a copy of the *Herald* that someone had left at the reception desk and trudged back up the stairs to his office. He had barely had chance to check if the statement he'd issued had been printed when there was an eager knock at his door.

"Yes, Jimmy!" he called out. His sergeant entered the office and Shadow frowned.

"How did you know I was back? You're not tracking my phone again, are you?"

Jimmy grinned and shook his head. "No, Chief, but I did ask reception to let me know when you arrived. I've got loads to report."

"Off you go then," said Shadow, leaning back in his chair as Jimmy flicked open his electronic notebook.

"Okay, first of all, trading standards phoned as soon as you'd left. They are going to pay Woodhouse and Ingham a visit."

"They'll struggle. Toby has closed for the day and Joe has disappeared apparently."

"What do you mean disappeared?"

"I don't know, but I do know that he's lied to us again. He was meant to be studying chemistry, not the classics."

"That's a weird lie to tell. How did you find out?"

"I was chatting to someone at Bacchus while Luca was talking to Oliver."

Jimmy started grinning.

"What's so funny?" asked Shadow.

"Nothing, Chief. It's just not like you to chat to people."

"I must have been working with you too long," retorted Shadow. "What else have you got to tell me?"

"Firstly, there's no connection between David Smith and Barbara Smith. I checked and her late husband was Geoff Smith. Then, I managed to get through to Inspector Grabowski. I asked her about David Smith. She was really surprised when I said he was dead, and even more interested when I explained that we thought his death might not be an accident."

"She knows him?" queried Shadow. "I thought he didn't have a record."

"This is where it gets a bit complicated, Chief. David Smith might not be David Smith. There's some dispute over his real name, but he's known by the guys in Grabowski's team as Mr Fixit."

"Not another daft name," complained Shadow as Jimmy continued to read from his notes.

"He's always been a bit dodgy but managed to stay on the right side of the law. He's set up a few companies that have been fronts for criminal organisations. Grabowski has been investigating a possible link between him and the Snowman's Albanian gang. They were seen together once by one of her surveillance teams. Inspector Grabowski thought the fact he doesn't have a record might be part of this appeal."

"Did you ask her about Don Rossetti?"

"Yes, she'd heard about him and was pretty surprised to think he was in York, but she didn't think the SCU were operating here. She is going to check with some colleagues in the DEA, in case they know anything."

Shadow groaned. He was not a fan of acronyms.

"Well, hopefully she'll come up with something that might help, but if it turns out the Sacra Corona Unita are involved, then we'll have to hand all our information over to the National Crime Agency or the drug enforcement lot anyway. Organised crime is their responsibility."

Jimmy looked disappointed.

"That's a shame. I was hoping we might have cracked the case before I go away on my honeymoon. If it turns out the SCU are responsible for killing Anna and Smith, I might even have got the chance to arrest a Mafia hitman."

Shadow snorted and gave a cynical shake of his head.

"I don't think that was ever a possibility, Sergeant. Professional killers go in and do what they need to do. They don't start faffing around splashing water on the floor and pretending their victim slipped or hit young women over the head with random stones. If they'd killed Anna, I doubt we'd have found her body so quickly."

CHAPTER EIGHT

Down 1 (9 letters)
Initially Zoe and Zelda meld with Bee to obtain funds fraudulently

THAT EVENING SHADOW and Luca were dining at La Scuola Femminile and Maggie was joining them. No sooner had they placed their order than Francesco had whisked Luca away to inspect the wine cellar beneath the restaurant.

"Do you happen to know a Barbara Smith?" asked Shadow as he topped up Maggie's glass of wine. She arched an eyebrow.

"The Black Widow? I thought I spotted you with her in Harkers earlier."

Shadow shook his head. He should have known better than to think his meeting would have gone unnoticed. Maggie was possibly the one person in York who was better informed than Barbara Smith.

"Why the Black Widow?" he asked.

"Well, for a start, I've never seen her wear any other colour and there aren't many women who have put three

162

husbands in the grave before they turn fifty," replied Maggie, spearing an olive with a cocktail stick before popping it into her mouth.

"She's been widowed three times?"

"Yes, her first husband, he was a lawyer named Taylor. He was killed in a car crash. The second one owned a chain of chemists. He was called Jones and he slipped and banged his head climbing out of the swimming pool at their villa in the South of France. Then last but not least came Geoff Smith; he's the one she inherited all her property from."

"What happened to him?"

"Dropped dead of a heart attack at the eighteenth hole of Ganton Golf Course."

"She was never implicated in their deaths though?" queried Shadow and he contemplated the choice of names of her husbands. Three of the most popular in the country and an excellent way for a woman born Rossetti to hide her true identity.

"No, I don't think so," replied Maggie, "but there wasn't a particularly long gap between husbands."

"I still think calling her the Black Widow is a bit harsh."

"Who is this Black Widow?" asked Luca, looking confused as he rejoined them at the table.

"Barbara Smith, the woman we saw this morning with Don Rossetti. She's his daughter," explained Shadow. "I spoke to her earlier."

"You must be careful, John," insisted Luca. "They are

dangerous people."

"You sound as bad Jimmy," muttered Shadow.

Maggie picked up her glass of wine. "That's enough talk about work. I want to hear all about Luca and his family, and you must tell me how to pronounce your wine again. It's absolutely delicious."

"Thank you, I am pleased you are enjoying it. It is called Greco Salice Salentino," replied Luca, enunciating the last three words slowly.

"Italian is such a beautiful language," said Maggie, waving her hand towards the menu on the table. "*Pollo picante* sounds so much nicer than spicy chicken."

"It does," agreed Luca with a slightly arrogant shrug. "I remember my English tutor used to joke that Giuseppe Verdi may not have been as successful or as popular if he'd been called Joe Green."

Maggie laughed. "That's probably true. I love *La Traviata*. I think it's my favourite opera."

"Then you have something in common with my dear sister, Luisa. It was also her favourite." Luca then launched into a loud rendition of Alfredo's brindisi from the opera, much to Maggie's delight and Shadow's embarrassment. He finished to applause from some of the surrounding tables.

"Luisa adored music and dancing," he explained a little breathlessly as he took a sip of wine. "She was always dancing, wasn't she, John?"

He turned to Shadow, who nodded, then shocked himself by saying, "Yes, every Friday we would go to a swing club, off Regent Street. They had an exceptional house band."

"Really?" said Maggie, looking even more surprised than he was. "I had no idea you could dance."

"For my part, it was more shuffling along in time to the music," he replied with a self-conscious shrug. Luca's way of talking about Luisa all the time was becoming infectious.

"In Lecce, in the summer, we have some wonderful festivals. Lots of music and dancing. You must both come," declared Luca.

"It sounds wonderful," said Maggie, while at the same time Shadow merely mumbled, "Perhaps."

"John doesn't often go on holiday," explained Maggie.

Luca nodded and leaning towards her, he whispered conspiratorially, "So I hear, but I am trying to get him to spend Christmas with us. I need all the help I can get."

Maggie grinned. "I'll try my best," she said, then turning to Shadow: "Have you really never been there since Luisa's funeral?"

Luca and Shadow exchanged a glance.

"I didn't go to her funeral," he admitted quietly.

Maggie stared at him. "Why not? When you said you'd never been to Italy, I assumed you meant on holiday. I had no idea you hadn't gone out there to lay her to rest."

There was an awkward pause and Shadow felt the blood rush to his face.

Luca cleared his throat. "You must understand, Maggie, it was a difficult time. My parents were upset," he began to explain, but Shadow held up his hand to interrupt him.

"It wasn't their fault. I could have gone, but I suppose I felt I didn't deserve to be there." He paused as the painful memory he always pushed away fought its way through. "I didn't say goodbye to her, you see. On the day she died, we'd overslept. The night before she'd talked me into staying up late to watch one of those old black-and-white films she loved. I woke up in a panic, knowing I would be late for work. Luisa woke up as I'd finished getting dressed and was heading to the door. She called my name from the bedroom. I should have gone back and kissed her, told her I loved, but instead I just said, 'Go back to sleep.' I'd taken her for granted. I think I was even a bit cross because I was late." He felt his voice catch in his throat. "If I couldn't take the time to say goodbye when she was alive, why should I be allowed to when she was gone?"

Maggie reached across the table and squeezed his hand, her eyes glistening with tears.

"You must not think like that, my friend," Luca, who was drying his own tears with a napkin, assured him. "Luisa knew you loved her."

At that moment, their food arrived and Shadow – relieved to have a distraction – lowered his head, but for once his appetite had deserted him.

The rest of the meal was spent listening to Luca tell stories about his family and his childhood. After dinner, Shadow and Maggie walked him to his hotel, then on the way back to Goodramgate, they took a detour through Dean's Park. It was usually closed to the public in the evening, but during St Nick's Fair it remained open with the trees decorated with fairy lights and stalls selling mince pies and the ubiquitous mulled wine.

"How much of that stuff can people drink?" grumbled Shadow as the scent of cinnamon and spices wafted around them.

"Perhaps it's a conspiracy. The city stall holders have banded together to annoy you," said Maggie, her lips curving into a smile.

"It certainly feels that way," replied Shadow.

Maggie took his arm and the two of them strolled along the path in silence, listening to the group of carol singers singing "Good King Wenceslas" outside the Minster library.

"Are you going to take Luca up on his offer?" she asked.

"Which offer?"

"To spend Christmas in Lecce with his family."

"Why would I do that?" replied Shadow gruffly.

"Oh, I don't know…because it will be sunny and at least ten degrees warmer out there than it is here. There'll be more Italian food and wine than even you know what to do with and you'll finally get to visit Luisa's final resting place."

"Luca was simply being polite," protested Shadow, while thinking that *final resting place* sounded so much nicer than grave.

"Admittedly I've only met him once, but he doesn't strike me as the sort of person who says things without meaning them."

By now they were walking past Minster Court. Shadow was trying to think of a way to ask Maggie if she would like to spend Christmas in Italy with him when he was distracted by the sound of tapping on glass. He looked up and saw Gwyneth Marchman watching them from an upstairs window in her house. Maggie smiled and waved back at her.

"Poor woman," she sighed as they passed by.

"Do you know her?"

"Oh yes, Gwyneth has been coming to me for years. It used to be for help getting wine stains out of Hugh's cassock, but since her accident she brings bedding and other larger items to the laundry."

"What happened to her?" asked Shadow.

"She fell down the steps that lead to the crypt beneath the Minster. Such a sad story. They'd only been here in York for a couple of years. I think she was carrying a large floral arrangement and she didn't notice that the door down to the crypt had been left open. She broke her spine. Hugh was devastated. He felt he should have taken better care of her."

Shadow nodded. He knew that feeling all too well.

"Has he always been the treasurer?" he asked.

"Yes, for years. He was very close to the previous dean. There was talk of him becoming dean himself one day, but after Gwyneth's accident, he put his own ambitions to one side and concentrated on looking after her."

"Does Gwyneth work?"

"Not anymore. She used to be a music teacher, travelling around the schools giving individual lessons in piano and singing. Funnily enough I was reminded of her when Luca talked about Verdi. Gwyneth loves all the classical stuff, especially the Italian composers. She was the one who first introduced me to opera. I didn't think it was my kind of thing, but she lent me a CD of *La Traviata* and I was hooked."

"But she doesn't work anymore?"

"No. She occasionally helps tutor some of the Minster choristers, but she would have needed a specially adapted car to let her travel around the city and, between you and me, I'm not sure they could afford it."

"Do they have children?"

Maggie shook her head. "No, I think they both wanted a family, but after her accident, well, I assumed that was no longer possible. Gwyneth doesn't talk about her private life much, but her face always lights up when she mentions Hugh. They send me a Christmas card every year and sign it individually. They both have beautiful handwriting. I remember her telling me that sitting down in the evenings and writing them is one of her favourite things about Christmas."

By now they were on Goodramgate and outside Maggie's

laundry.

"How long are you planning on staying here in the flat?" asked Shadow. Earlier in the year Maggie had moved out of her cottage when the remains of Roman gladiators had been found in her garden.

"I'm not sure, but I can't see me ever moving home again. It gives me the creeps just thinking about it," she replied with a shudder. "Actually, I've rented it out to two of the archaeologists who were working on the dig while I decide what to do. Sam is always badgering me to move out to Spain to be near him, at least for part of the year."

"You're thinking of leaving York?" asked Shadow, surprised at how upset he felt at the thought.

Maggie shrugged. "Maybe. We'll see."

She reached up and kissed him gently on the cheek. "Thank you for a lovely evening and I'm pleased I met Luca. It was nice to hear about Luisa. It's a shame you don't share your memories of her more often."

Shadow stood on the pavement as Maggie let herself into the laundry, waited for a moment until he saw a light in the window of the upper floor and then he turned and began to walk towards Petergate. The cold was stinging his cheeks. It was the first time he'd noticed the temperature that night. He turned the corner and stopped. In one of the shop doorways sat Jamie and Kayleigh and kneeling down to talk to them was Joe Ingham.

"It gladdens your heart to see such charity, doesn't it,

Chief Inspector?" said a voice behind him. He turned to see Clarissa Fortescue smiling broadly at him. "I often see that young man providing hot drinks to those in need. He's a credit to his generation."

Shadow thought it best not to give his opinion on what he thought Joe Ingham might be up to and instead nodded to Simon Fortescue, who was a few paces behind his wife and laden down with bags and parcels.

"Christmas shopping?" enquired Shadow.

"Yes, indeed, Chief Inspector," replied Clarissa. "There simply aren't enough hours in the day, so late-night opening is an absolute blessing."

Shadow wasn't sure her husband felt the same. He certainly looked more subdued than the first time he'd seen him and there were dark circles beneath his eyes.

"May I ask if you've received any more anonymous letters?" he asked the dean, wondering if this was what was causing her husband to worry, but Clarissa shook her head firmly.

"No, Chief Inspector, I'm pleased to say that particular unpleasantness seems to have come to an end. Perhaps the writer grew bored or they realised that this is meant to be the season of goodwill. I'm certainly feeling rather festive now and there's nothing like spending Christmas in a city to make it feel like home. We even found time to pop into Bettys for a spot of supper after we'd finished shopping, so I almost feel like a local," continued Clarissa. "I really can't remember when we last had such a fun and busy evening. I'm quite exhausted."

"Then I won't keep you any longer," replied Shadow, noting that Simon Fortescue hadn't said a word. "Good evening."

Shadow turned back towards the doorway as the Fortescues headed back towards the Minster, but Jamie, Kayleigh and Joe were nowhere to be seen. He shook his head as he continued on his way. He would have liked to speak to the young man, but at least now he knew he was still in the city somewhere.

He plunged his hands in his pockets, hoping to locate an indigestion tablet, but instead found the last poison pen letter and Marjorie's photocopy of the wine receipt. Until now, he'd forgotten all about them.

THE NEXT MORNING, Shadow was standing in the incident room, staring at the whiteboard covered with photos and annotations, wondering if the pieces of this particular puzzle would ever fit together, when Jimmy came bounding into the room.

"Guess what, Chief?"

"Surely you know by now I don't play guessing games, Sergeant."

"I've found out something that could be pretty interesting. Last night, I was in bed reading – remember I told you about the book Sophie bought me about the gangs in Europe?"

Shadow nodded as he wondered how long it would take his sergeant to get to the point.

"I was hoping to find out more about Rossetti and the SCU," continued Jimmy, "when I suddenly remembered that library book you found in Anna's flat. Well, I thought she must have been a member, so I called in this morning to tell them about the book and see if anyone there knew her."

"And?"

"As luck would have it June was on duty and remembered her really well. She said she was a really lovely girl, so polite and interested in what June had to say. Like Jake said, she preferred mysteries, but was happy to read different genre and June said she never returned a book late."

"Hang on, who is this June person?"

"Oh, you must remember June, Chief. She was one of the volunteers at the Roman museum. We interviewed her when those old coins had been stolen."

Shadow shook his head. He could vaguely recall a long line of elderly ladies and gentlemen, dozing or knitting as they waited in a corridor for Jimmy to question them, but nobody specific. However, it was more than likely his overly friendly sergeant now received Christmas cards from each and every one of them.

"Well," continued Jimmy, "June also volunteers at the

library Thursdays and Fridays and Friday was the day Anna always visited."

"Any particular reason for Fridays?"

"I'm getting to that, Chief. You see Fridays are quite special at the library. They run an outreach programme. On Friday afternoons, a professional comes to read a chapter of one of the classics – you know Charles Dickens or Jane Austen or something."

"I am aware of the classic writers in English literature, Sergeant," Shadow groaned. "This is like getting blood out of a stone! Will you get to the point?"

"Yes, Chief. The professional reader is Simon Fortescue. He's been doing it for quite a few months now. Apparently, Anna never missed one of his readings and according to June, well, to quote her, 'He paid Anna more attention than a married man should.'"

Shadow raised his eyebrows. "So you think Anna could be the mystery woman Webster saw Fortescue with?"

"It sounds like it, Chief. She would certainly fit the description he gave us and remember her diary had lots of SFs in it. We thought it was La Scuola Femminile, but it could be Simon Fortescue." Jimmy was grinning broadly, but Shadow wasn't entirely convinced.

"Let's be sure. I want Webster to take a look at Anna's photo," he said, standing up and removing her picture from the whiteboard and handing it to his sergeant.

The two detectives left the station and headed over to St

William's College.

"Hey, Chief, do you know what else June told me? She and her husband are about to celebrate their fifty-fifth wedding anniversary and the two of them still go dancing every weekend. Isn't that great?"

"Wonderful, but what's it got to do with the investigation?"

"Well, nothing, Chief, but it did sort of restore my faith in marriage, you know after hearing about Mr Fortescue cheating on the dean and poor hen-pecked Neville Prentis."

AS THEY APPROACHED the college, they almost bumped into Malcolm Webster, who was leaving the building at great speed, dressed in a black cloak and fedora.

"My apologies, gentlemen, but I cannot grant you an audience at this time," he declared theatrically. "Already I am late. The good ladies of the Knaresborough and District Women's Institute have requested my services. I am to act as their guide as they tour our fair city."

"This won't take a second. Please could you have a quick look at this picture for us, Mr Webster?" asked Jimmy, producing the photo of Anna from his inside pocket.

Webster took the photo and squinted as he held it at arm's length.

"Ah, I see like a modern-day Lord Elgin, you have discovered the image of Aphrodite, Sergeant," he said, kissing the tips of his fingers. "*Bellissimo!*"

"Is it the young woman you saw with Simon Fortescue in Harrogate or not?" asked Shadow, unable to hide his impatience.

"It is indeed, Chief Inspector. I would be prepared to stake my life on it."

"That won't be necessary, Mr Webster, but we may ask you to make a statement sometime in the future."

"I'm always ready and willing to carry out my civic duty, gentlemen. But for now, I must wish you farewell."

He handed the photo back to Jimmy, flung his cloak around him and strode away towards the Minster.

"Should we go and speak to Mr Fortescue?" asked Jimmy.

"Not yet. Let's give him a chance to come to us. If he cared about Anna and isn't involved in her death, then he must be concerned. If he's approached anyone at the hotel or Francesco and Lucia's place, then he'll have found out what has happened to her," replied Shadow. "Have her name and photo been released to the press yet?"

"Not yet, Chief. Francesco made the formal identification with Tom. He passed the information on via the local police, but her parents asked us to wait a few days. Her little sister is away on a school trip apparently and they don't want her to find out through social media before they have a chance to tell her themselves," explained Jimmy as they made their way back to the station. Shadow nodded, his thoughts straying to another set of parents who still had a teenager at home when they heard about the death of their daughter in a foreign country. Jimmy, however, leapt straight into voicing his theories about what this latest revelation might mean.

"Do you think Fortescue could have killed her, Chief? Maybe she threatened to tell his wife and he panicked? The basement of La Dolce Vita could have been where they met. It's not a very romantic place, is it? They couldn't very well have used Anna's flat, not with Marjorie Prentis being so close. She would be bound to have noticed something. Hang on though, wasn't Fortescue at the hospital with the dean on Sunday night?"

"Yes, he was," said Shadow, "he was there until eleven o'clock and according to the dean, when he returned home, he took a sleeping pill."

Jimmy's shoulders sank in disappointment.

"Then I guess it can't be him, Chief. It's a shame for us, but it would have broken the dean's heart to lose him."

THEY HAD BARELY set foot back in the station when Tom came hurrying towards them.

"The chief constable called for you, Chief. She said to tell you she's emailed you and expects a response within the hour."

"Why can't she just ask me to ring her back like a normal person?" muttered Shadow.

"To be fair, I think by now she's probably realised that doesn't work, Chief," replied Jimmy as he trotted up the stairs after his boss. The two of them arrived at Shadow's office and he went through the unfamiliar procedure of turning on his computer and checking his emails. There at the top of an extensive list, marked urgent, was the one from Chief Constable Maxwell. Shadow opened it and quickly scanned the contents.

"She's heard that we've been asking about the Sacra Corona Unita and David Smith, 'a known associate of a prominent Albanian criminal' as she puts it. She wants a video conference between her, us and Inspector Grabowski tomorrow morning. She's expecting a full briefing apparently."

"Why is she suddenly so interested? She's never asked us to have a video conference before," asked Jimmy.

Shadow began half-heartedly typing his response using only his index finger.

"If there's any chance of North Yorkshire Police being connected to a major investigation the chief constable will want to make sure she's involved. She's an ambitious lady. I expect she'd like to move to a larger force at some point and having her name connected to the National Crime Agency won't do her any harm. It sounds very much as though we shall have to hand the case over to Inspector Grabowski and her team."

Having pressed send, Shadow rose to his feet and collected his jacket from the back of his chair.

"Can I leave you to prepare for the meeting, Sergeant?"

Jimmy looked at him in surprise. "You want me to brief Inspector Grabowski and Chief Constable Maxwell?"

"Why not? You know the case as well as I do, and more importantly, you know all the jargon the chief constable likes to hear. Besides, I'm having lunch with Luca. He's going back to Italy this evening."

"Sure. No problem, Chief," replied Jimmy, but his expression had become unusually serious and he couldn't quite look Shadow in the eye.

"Is there something you want to say, Sergeant?" asked Shadow.

Jimmy sighed heavily, putting down the pen, then picking it up again. "It's just that I've been thinking, Chief."

"What about?"

"Luca. I mean he seems really nice, but we don't know a lot about him. It was his wine that started all this off and it was him who told us about Barbara and her father. You first phoned him on his mobile. We assumed he was at home, but for all we know he could have already been in the country. Maybe he is connected to criminals back in Italy. Then, you mentioned the case of the ghost walk guys. They were killed out of revenge. What happens if Luca still holds a grudge about what happened to his sister after all? Maybe he wants to get at you somehow or thinks you won't suspect him because of his connection to Luisa. I don't know, but you don't really know him, and you've accepted everything he's told you…" Jimmy trailed off and glanced anxiously at his boss. "I'm really sorry if I've overstepped the mark. Are you angry, Chief?"

Shadow stared silently at the younger man for a moment, then slowly shook his head.

"No, I'm just a little surprised. I'm not used to you being more suspicious than me. Maybe we really have been working together too long. For what it's worth, I don't think Luca is involved, but you are right: it's possible my judgement is clouded. Check with the airlines and find out what flight he was on."

"Yes, Chief," replied Jimmy, looking relieved as Shadow turned and left the office.

HE HAD ARRANGED to meet Luca for lunch on *Florence*. Luca may have been a little surprised when Shadow told him he still lived on the narrow boat, but he was keen to see his sister's last home. He had insisted on providing lunch and came laden down with cold meats, olives, focaccia and wine from Catania's.

"It is good of you to make time to see me when you are so busy," he said as he filled Shadow's glass.

"Not at all. I've enjoyed you being here, and besides it looks like the case I was working on may soon be handed to another team."

Luca raised his own glass in a toast. "To you, Chief Inspector Shadow. Luisa would be very proud of you achieving such a high rank."

Shadow shifted in embarrassment. "It's probably due to her that I am a chief inspector. When I lost her, work was all I had to think about."

"Why did you not stay in London? Surely that would have been the best thing for your career."

"Too many memories," replied Shadow simply.

Luca glanced around the boat. "This place looks exactly as it did in the photos Luisa sent home, although there would have been more flowers if she were still here." He pointed to one of the few cushions on the sofa. "I even remember my mother sending that cushion cover over. If I may say so, my friend, it seems like you brought all your memories with you. Perhaps it is time to move on."

Shadow stared at the younger man for a few seconds, but the anger and irritation he used to feel when anyone suggested something similar didn't materialise.

"Perhaps you are right," he conceded, taking another sip of wine.

LUCA WAS TAKING a flight from Leeds Bradford Airport back to Italy that evening. After lunch, Shadow accompanied him to his hotel, which took longer than expected as Luca insisted on calling into several shops along the way to do some Christmas shopping. It was growing dark when Shadow finally loaded him, his suitcase, several bulging shopping bags and an oversized teddy bear into a taxi. With a final promise to keep in touch, Shadow waved him off. He watched as the taxi pulled away, then he turned up the collar of his coat and headed down towards the Minster. He'd decided it was time to pay Simon Fortescue a visit.

SHADOW WAS A little surprised when the dean herself opened the front door of the Deanery.

"Good evening, Chief Inspector. This is a nice surprise. Or should I be worried?"

"Not at all, but I hoped to have a word with Mr Fortescue," said Shadow as he stepped into the large hallway.

"It's nothing I can help you with?"

"I'm afraid not. It's regarding his voluntary work at the library. We are investigating the death of a young woman who attending his readings," explained Shadow, closely watching the dean's reaction.

"Oh, how awful. Not the young woman you recovered from the river? I read about it in the paper."

Shadow nodded.

"Such a tragedy. I'm sure Simon will do anything he can to assist you. Come though into the drawing room, Chief Inspector. He shouldn't be too long. He was at the faculty's Christmas drinks, but he texted a few minutes ago to say he's on his way."

Shadow followed her into an elegantly proportioned room with a polished wooden floor and a roaring open fire. There was a large Christmas tree in front of the French doors with countless presents stacked beneath. The dean gestured to one of the large sofas, scattered with tapestry cushions. Shadow took a seat while Clarissa moved over to the oak sideboard where there was a silver tray holding several bottles and glasses.

"Will you join me in a sherry while you wait, Chief Inspector?" she asked.

"Thank you," replied Shadow, glancing around the room. "How are you settling in?"

"It's beginning to feel like home. Mainly thanks to Simon. I'm afraid I tend to leave all the unpacking and so forth to him. It's been the same since I was ordained. Whenever I moved to a new parish, I'm so busy adapting to the job, poor Simon is left to sort things out on the home front as it were. It may be for the best; he has a much better eye for interior design than me, but I'm not sure it's what he bargained for when we married thirty years ago."

"How did the two of you meet?"

"At university. We were both members of the drama society."

"Did you want to act too?"

Clarissa shook her head and gave a wry smile. "No, Chief Inspector. I took part in school productions, but I was at an all girls' school and due to my height and build, I was always cast in the male roles. By the time I reached university I knew my limits. I was mainly involved backstage. Costumes, scenery, make-up, that sort of thing. The limelight was left to shine on those with real talent like Simon." She paused and handed Shadow his drink. "Although, there are some who say all members of the clergy are frustrated thespians. After all, every Sunday the Lord grants us a captive audience. Perhaps there is some truth in it. To your good health."

"And yours." Shadow raised his glass to hers. "Do you miss your life in London?" he asked.

"Not one bit, Chief Inspector." She took a sip of her sherry. "Simon and I see a lot more of each other now I'm not chained to my computer screen for twelve hours a day, but I think sometimes he misses the city. He's always needed excitement and glamour and I understand that."

Before Shadow could reply the front door closed with a bang and Simon's voice came echoing through from the hallway.

"Clarissa darling, I'm home. Where are you?"

"In here, darling," replied the dean, rising to her feet as her husband came through the door. He stopped for a second when he saw Shadow before kissing his wife on the cheek.

"Hello, Chief Inspector. Has something happened?"

Clarissa replied before Shadow could.

"Nothing to worry about, darling. Mr Shadow wanted to ask you about Miss Novak, who attended your reading group. It's the poor girl they found in the river. I'll leave the two of you to chat. I'll be in my office if you need me." And with that she was gone. As the door closed behind his wife, Simon Fortescue, his cheeks red from coming in from the cold, crossed the room in a few paces and poured himself a large whisky before turning to look at Shadow.

"I won't insult your intelligence by pretending I didn't know Anna, Chief Inspector."

"Thank you. That would certainly save us both time."

"I still can't believe she's gone," said Simon, sinking down on to the sofa opposite Shadow. "She'd tried to contact me on Sunday, but my stupid phone was broken, so on Monday morning, I went down and hung about outside the shop where she worked as a cleaner, but there was no sign of her. Then I read that you'd found a body. Who could have done such a thing? She was such a sweet girl. It broke my heart to think I might have been able to go to her aid, save her, instead of knocking myself out with a sleeping pill."

He ran his hand across his face.

"When did you last see her?" asked Shadow, watching him closely, knowing he was dealing with a professional actor.

"On Friday at the library. That's where I first met her. It was only my second week there. I was reading from Conan Doyle's *The Hound of the Baskervilles*. It turned out it was one of her favourite books. I looked up and there she was smiling back at me and all of a sudden it was as if the rest of the room had disappeared." Simon took a slug of whisky. "She wanted to see me on Saturday. She was upset about something, but I couldn't get away. On Sunday, she'd texted me a few times, but I'd left my phone in the vestry during the ceremony and then Clarissa was taken ill and in all the confusion, I left it behind and it got smashed."

"Did your wife know about your relationship with her?" asked Shadow.

Simon took another drink before answering. "Clarissa has always been very understanding about these things."

"So, Anna wasn't your first extramarital affair?"

"It's the excitement, you see," explained Simon, as if he hadn't heard Shadow's question. "Life can be so dull, especially since we left London. Then to suddenly find yourself in the middle of a wonderful romance. The centre of a beautiful young woman's world. I owe Clarissa so much…" He trailed off and knocked back the rest of his whisky, then immediately stood up and went over to the sideboard for a refill. Shadow glanced around the elegant room. Simon was right. Clarissa may no longer be earning the sort of salary she did as an accountant, but thanks to her, Simon lived in one of the best houses in the city, something that would never have been possible for a part-time lecturer at the university.

With a full glass, Simon leaned back against the sideboard and began speaking again. "You see, Chief Inspector, Clarissa doesn't really need me. She never has. I'm only part of her supporting cast. With Anna it was different. She needed me, wanted me. I was her hero. Her leading man." He took another drink. "We even discussed running away together. Back to Slovenia or even Italy."

Privately, Shadow thought Simon Fortescue was a little too old to consider running away but didn't comment.

"What was Anna worried about?" he asked instead.

"She wouldn't tell me. She said if she was right, it was better I didn't know. She wanted to protect me." His voice cracked. "I should never have taken that stupid sleeping pill. The last text I received from her on Sunday…she said that everything would be all right after Monday and that it would be a relief not to have to keep a secret. I replied that I thought that was wonderful and asked if she wanted to see me after the Advent Procession, but I never received her reply."

"Did you manage to get your phone fixed?"

Simon opened his mouth to answer, but at that moment, there was the sound of breaking glass and a muffled scream. Shadow and Simon both sprang to their feet and dashed out of the drawing room across the hall and into the dean's study. Clarissa was standing in front of the French doors, her hand over her mouth as she stared in horror at the shards of glass scattered over the rug by her feet.

"Darling, are you all right? What happened?" asked Simon, rushing over to his wife.

"I was sitting at my desk reading when that came flying through the door," said Clarissa in a shaking voice. She pointed to a lump of stone lying amongst the glass.

"Did you see anybody out in the garden?" asked Shadow, using his handkerchief to stoop and retrieve it.

"No, and all the gates are locked. Whoever it was must have been standing on the city walls," said the dean, resting her head against her husband's shoulder.

Shadow immediately went to the French doors. They were unlocked. He stepped out into the terrace. It was dark, but the city walls were illuminated and there was no sign of anyone on the stretch that overlooked the rear gardens of the Deanery. Turning the stone over in his hand, he saw that it did indeed look like it could be a piece of loose masonry from the walls. He glanced over his shoulder. The dean's desk was a little to the left of the French doors. There was a bright table lamp on the corner of the desk and a warm glow coming from the open fire. From outside the dean would have been clearly visible. He took a few moments to wander around the gardens deep in thought.

"You are right: the garden gates are locked and there is no sign of an intruder trying to get in. Would you like me to send a uniformed officer over?" he asked as he stepped back into the study.

"No, Chief Inspector. Thank you, but no. It was probably mischievous children playing a prank. Except for a broken pane of glass there's no harm done."

"Are you sure, darling?" asked Simon, who was carefully picking up the broken glass.

"Absolutely, Simon."

"Then I'll wish you both a good night," replied Shadow. "I'll show myself out."

CHAPTER NINE

Down 7 (7 letters)
An ace coin is needed to buy an illicit drug

S HADOW WALKED AWAY from the Deanery with a hundred thoughts jostling for position in his head. As he approached the Minster, he saw George pulling on his gloves as he walked across the car park. He raised his hand in greeting when he saw Shadow.

"Evening, John. What brings you here?"

"I was paying a visit to the Deanery. Have you got time for a pint?"

"Always," agreed George.

The Cross Keys was only a few steps away. George waved hello to several other drinkers as he went to find a table in the corner, while Shadow ordered two pints of Black Sheep. Placing the two glasses on the table, he took a seat opposite his old friend.

"So, what do you want to pick my brains about?" asked George.

"I wanted to ask you about the night of the Advent ceremony."

George looked at him in surprise.

"Are you still looking into that business with the dean? I thought you'd have enough on your plate with that poor girl you found in the river."

"It's looking like we might have to hand that case over to the National Crime Agency, but I've been wondering if there's a chance there could be a connection between the girl we found and what happened at the Minster," explained Shadow a little cagily. He didn't want to start discussing Simon's affair with Anna in a crowded pub. "Where were you before the ceremony started? I didn't see you until afterwards."

"I was by the door of the vestry. That's where all the choristers, the clergy, everyone taking part in the procession was getting ready, putting on their robes and so forth. I was making sure that nobody went in who wasn't meant to, then when they'd all come out, I locked the door after them. Everyone involved had to leave their valuables like handbags and phones in there, you see. They used to ask for the phones to be turned off, but someone – usually one of the youngsters – would always forget. When the ceremony started, I stood by one of the emergency exits until the end, then I unlocked the door again."

"Where was Simon Fortescue during the ceremony?" asked Shadow.

George gave him a quizzical look. "He was taking part in the ceremony. He was one of the candle bearers, along with

Marjorie and a couple of the teachers from the Minster school. They were the ones dressed in white who lit all the candles."

"What happened at the end of the ceremony?"

"I unlocked the door, and everyone went to get changed."

"Wait, they all get changed together?"

"It's only the outer ceremonial vestments they remove like the copes and albs."

Shadow nodded. "Who was the last person to leave the vestry?"

"The dean herself," replied George promptly.

"You sound very sure."

George looked a little embarrassed as he took a sip of his pint and lowered his voice. "Well, you see I was wanting them all to hurry up. I was desperate for the loo and there's a staff toilet next to the vestry, but it was occupied by Canon Marchman. He went straight there after the ceremony and was in for ages."

"Perhaps he wasn't well."

"No, it was nothing like that. I could hear the tap running from outside. At first, I thought he must have burnt his hand on a candle and was running it under cold water, but when he came out, he was carrying his stole, the narrow strip of cloth he wore draped around his neck, and he was looking even more worried than usual. I asked him if he was all right and he said he'd been trying to wash a dirty mark out of the stole."

"What sort of dirty mark?"

"I didn't ask, but I understood him being worried. Marjorie is in charge of all the ceremonial vestments and woe betide anyone who damages or dirties them. She's had at least three of the young choristers in tears over grubby marks on their surplices."

Shadow nodded. He could well believe it. The woman had even turned her own husband into a nervous wreck.

"So, what happened next?"

"Canon Marchman must have removed his outer vestments in the loo and handed them straight to Marjorie, who had already noticed they weren't with the others. She put them in the vestry, then she and the dean left at the same time. I put my head around the door to check everyone had gone. Then I locked up and finally managed to go to the loo."

"What happened with Simon Fortescue's phone?"

"He must have forgotten to collect it after the ceremony. I unlocked the vestry for Marjorie the next morning and there it was on the floor, under one of the tables with the screen all smashed. Now enough of work. What are you up to over Christmas?"

Half an hour later, after Shadow had heard all about the toy train set George had bought for his grandson, they left the pub. Shadow said goodbye to his old friend, but instead of following him down Goodramgate, he turned in the opposite direction and walked towards Monk Bar. He read the notice pinned to the locked wooden door at the bottom of the narrow stone steps and nodded to himself. His memory was correct.

WHEN HE ARRIVED at the station the next morning, Shadow found the incident room had been rearranged for the video meeting with Chief Constable Maxwell and Inspector Grabowski. The whiteboards had been moved to make space for two large screens. Shadow reluctantly took his seat next to Jimmy, who was positioned in front of a camera. His sergeant kept clearing his throat, straightening his tie and was nervously checking through his notes. Shadow briefly updated him on what he'd learnt from Simon Fortescue the previous night and Jimmy hurriedly scribbled it all down.

"By the way, Chief. I checked out Luca. He was definitely on the flight he told you about," he said.

"As I suspected," replied Shadow, nodding to Tom, who was sitting directly behind them. The young constable had been rather subdued since the mix-up with contacting the police from Anna's home country. Inspector Grabowski, who Shadow had briefly met once earlier in the year, appeared on one of the screens along with several other plain-clothed officers. The letters ROCU were written on the wall behind her. Jimmy was engrossed in his notes, so Shadow turned to Tom.

"I thought she was from the National Crime Agency?"

"She was," replied Tom. "She transferred to the Regional Organised Crime Unit in Leeds a few months ago. I guess it made sense to have her as the link between the Yorkshire and Humber regional forces and the NCA."

Shadow nodded and sighed. He hated acronyms and abbreviations and he had a feeling this meeting was going to be full of them.

Jimmy rose to his feet as Chief Constable Maxwell appeared on her screen from her office at North Yorkshire Police's headquarters in Northallerton. After she'd welcomed them all to the meeting, she handed over to him. Shadow listened as Jimmy gave a clear and concise update on everything that had happened since their first visit to La Dolce Vita. Inspector Grabowski seemed to be making notes and the chief constable nodded her head occasionally. She was the first to speak when Jimmy had finished.

"Thank you, Sergeant Chang. As I suspected, this appears to be an extremely complex case that may call on us to involve both the DEA…"

"Drug Enforcement Agency," Tom whispered behind Shadow.

"…and HMRC…"

"Her Majesty's Revenue and Customs, Chief," hissed Tom.

"Yes, thank you. I know that one, Tom," Shadow hissed

back as the chief constable continued to speak.

"But it would be quite something if ROCU working alongside the NYP were responsible for breaking a drugs ring with Don Rossetti at the centre."

Inspector Grabowski raised her hand. "Excuse me, ma'am, but we haven't received any intelligence that would lead us to believe that the Sacra Corona Unita are operating in Yorkshire, or indeed anywhere in the UK," said Inspector Grabowski. "What's more, my opposite number in the Lecce Police agrees with the information we received from Chief Inspector Shadow. He's heard from various sources that Don Rossetti had retired to this country to be with his daughter. There was a rumour that he is in the early stages of dementia and was seen as a liability."

Shadow nodded as he recalled Barbara's comment about her father liking to tell stories from the past. Something not unusual to people suffering from that the disease, but not a very safe trait for a gangster to develop.

Inspector Grabowski pressed on. "Here at the ROCU we would like to continue with our investigation into the Albanian gang who we believe are behind the drugs supply in Leeds. We are looking into a possible connection between Smith and the man we only know as the Snowman, ma'am."

The chief constable shook her head firmly. "No, I don't believe men like Don Rossetti ever retire, Inspector. I'm convinced he must be behind the supply of drugs in York and by extension the murders of David Smith and Anna

Novak. It's too much of a coincidence that the head of an organised crime family arrived in the city and all this happens."

Shadow could tell from Inspector Grabowski's expression that she was as unconvinced as he was by this course of action, but she wasn't about to contradict the chief constable, who was still speaking.

"I want the ROCU to start tapping the telephones of Barbara Smith and to organise a surveillance operation, in let's say twenty-four hours. Also, investigate again any connection between her and David Smith. Their names seem too much of a coincidence too. Then I want CSI to take a look at the hotel room Smith was found in and this wine shop. Have the young men who work there been seen recently, Sergeant Chang?"

"No, ma'am," replied Jimmy. "There's no sign of them and the place has been closed since trading standards contacted them."

"I want you to double-check the alibi they have for Sunday night," ordered the chief constable.

Shadow folded his arms turned to look out the window as his boss continued to suggest courses of action that they had either already followed or ruled as unnecessary. He watched as large powdery flakes of snow began falling from the sky. It looked like Sophie would get her wish of a white wedding, while over in Lecce it was sunny and fifteen degrees. He'd checked the European weather in the newspaper that morning.

The chief constable paused and switched her steely gaze to Jimmy. "Thank you for your input, Sergeant Chang. I would have asked the ROCU to liaise with you, but I understand you'll be away for several weeks following your marriage tomorrow." Then almost as an afterthought she said, "Congratulations."

"Thank you, ma'am," replied Jimmy, smiling politely while sounding slightly deflated.

The meeting ended and both Chief Constable Maxwell and Inspector Grabowski disappeared from their screens. Jimmy slapped his notes down on the table and shook his head in disappointment.

"So, that's it, Chief. The whole investigation has been taken away from us. It feels like we've wasted our time this last week."

Shadow got to his feet and patted the younger man on the shoulder.

"Don't let it bother you too much, Sergeant. Like the chief constable said, you'll be off on your honeymoon tomorrow and it wasn't all a waste of time. You did an excellent job with the briefing. You'll have made a good impression on Inspector Grabowski and Chief Constable Maxwell."

"Thanks, Chief," replied Jimmy, looking up in surprise at his uncharacteristic compliment.

Shadow spent the rest of the afternoon preparing reports

to be handed over to Inspector Grabowski and her team, as requested by the chief constable. Outside his window snowflakes continued to fall from the leaden sky. He stood up for a moment to watch as they were swallowed by the swirling and churning Ouse. He couldn't help thinking his time would be better spent investigating the death of the young woman they'd pulled out of there only a few days earlier. Instead, it looked like she was going to be treated as collateral damage, only a small part of the bigger drugs investigation everyone seemed so obsessed with. The chief constable had barely shown any interest when Jimmy had given details of her working and private life.

At exactly five o'clock that evening Shadow and Jimmy left the station together. Jimmy still seemed a little subdued.

"Cheer up," said Shadow. "You are away for three weeks from tomorrow, so you wouldn't have been around for the investigation anyway. You've got more important things to think about."

It was the night before the wedding and Rose, Jimmy's mother, was hosting a dinner for all the members of her family who had arrived in the city from Hong Kong. Shadow had been invited too.

"Isn't it more traditional to have your stag do the night before the wedding?" he queried as they ploughed their way through the endless throng of shoppers surrounding the wood huts on Parliament Street.

"Sophie and I had a joint do at the end of October. We

went go-karting and paintballing. Sophie combined the words 'hen' and 'stag' and called it a 'hag do', you know with it being near Halloween. We thought it was safer to hold it early in case of injuries. Neither of us wanted to appear on the wedding photos with a black eye. Don't you remember, Chief? You came to the meal afterwards at the Bengal Brasserie?"

Shadow grunted. He vaguely recalled being dragged along by Maggie to an Indian restaurant where the food played havoc with his digestive system. The heat of the food was matched only by the flaming shots Sophie and her brothers started downing at the end of the meal. Shadow hadn't stayed long.

As soon as they entered the Golden Dragon, Jimmy disappeared into a crowd of cheering and clapping relatives. Upstairs in the restaurant, a huge buffet table stretched out for the full length of the room and there were chairs loosely grouped together, although most people seemed to be happy to stand and eat and chat. Rose had provided enough food to feed an army. Shadow watched from his seat in the corner as she and Angela dashed back and forth ensuring all their guests had a full glass, pausing only to exchange a joke or a quick peck on the cheek.

His thoughts strayed to Luca. He would be back home in Italy now, ensconced with his own family. No doubt telling them all about his trip and the man they only knew from photos, who still lived on the boat he had shared with their aunt.

Jimmy's grandfather didn't appear to be particularly impressed by being surrounded by his extended family. As soon as the meal was over, Shadow felt a tap on his shoulder and the old man beckoned him over for their usual game of backgammon and as usual he lost.

When Shadow finally left the Golden Dragon, he didn't immediately head back to *Florence*, but instead made his way to Minster Court. The chief constable might have told him to take a step back from the investigation, but there was still one aspect he might be able to get to the bottom of.

"I APOLOGISE FOR the late hour, Mrs Marchman, but I was hoping to speak with your husband," he explained when Gwyneth answered the door.

"Do come in, Chief Inspector. No need to apologise. This isn't late to me. I'm a terrible insomniac. I don't usually retire until the early hours of the morning."

"I'm sorry – that must be very difficult for you," replied Shadow as he stepped into the hallway and closed the front door behind him.

"Oh, I'm used to it, Chief Inspector. Ever since my accident it's been this way. I put it down to not using up as much energy as when I was more mobile. I used to sleep like a log back then, but at least I'm not alone. I often see Simon, our new neighbour, taking a midnight stroll. He cuts such a dashing figure in that trilby," explained Gwyneth as she wheeled herself down a corridor. The Marchmans' house felt warm and cosy. The air was scented with coffee and fresh baking. Carols were playing softly in the background.

"Have you seen him recently?" he asked, noticing the framed opera and ballet programmes that lined the walls of the hallway.

"Oh yes, he's passed my window the last few nights."

"On Sunday night? After the Advent ceremony?"

"Yes. Hugh and I both heard the ambulance bringing Clarissa back, then an hour or so later, Hugh was asleep by then, but I saw Simon quite clearly in the distance. Not that I was too surprised. It must have been a terrible shock, poor man; no wonder he couldn't sleep."

By now they were outside a panelled door. Gwyneth pushed it open.

"Please wait here in Hugh's office, Chief Inspector. He's baking in the kitchen, attempting a panettone, bless him. He knows it's my favourite. I'll let him know you are here. He won't be a moment. May I offer you a cup of tea?"

"No, but thank you very much, Mrs Marchman," replied Shadow as he stepped into the tidy, but slightly shabby office.

Gwyneth wheeled herself back down the hallway calling out, "Hugh, Chief Inspector Shadow is here to see you, my dear."

Shadow glanced around the room. On the desk there was a sheaf of papers, a black fountain pen and a leather-bound Bible with several pieces of paper marking places in the Old Testament. He carefully opened it and fished out his glasses. He scanned through the text and shook his head. It was as he'd suspected. Gently he closed the Bible again as the door opened and Canon Marchman hurried in. He was wearing his usual anxious expression and an apron covered in jolly-looking robins over his dark suit and his hands were still covered with flour.

"Good heavens, Chief Inspector, is something wrong?" he asked, wiping his hand on the apron several times before offering it to the Chief Inspector.

"There's a matter I would like to discuss with you, Canon Marchman. Two matters, in fact."

Hugh's face turned as white as his hands. "Two matters, Chief Inspector?"

"Yes, Canon Marchman. Which would you like to begin with, the threatening letters you have been sending to the dean or the money you have been embezzling from the Minster?"

Hugh removed his glasses and collapsed into the armchair by the fire. "I've been an utter fool, Chief Inspector." He put his head in his hands and began to weep quietly. "I've risked everything for the sake of a few thousand pounds. Money truly is the root of all evil."

"I assume the letters were some sort of attempt to scare

off the new dean? With her background in accountancy, it was quite possible she would want to cast a professional eye over the accounts and find out what you'd been up to."

"I was desperate," Hugh sobbed. "Ever since I heard Clarissa had been appointed I've barely slept a wink. After twenty years as the canon treasurer, I'm trusted implicitly by the annual auditors. When her appointment was announced, a few letters turned up, complaining that it was against God's will to have a woman in that position. That's what gave me the idea. I only wanted to make her feel unwelcome. Everyone said she was destined to be a bishop. I thought I might be able to hasten her on."

Shadow removed the letter that was left at the Minster on the night of the Advent Procession from his pocket and placed it in front of the canon.

"You even left this one for her on the night of the Advent Procession, when you were in such a hurry you got ink on your vestments."

Hugh shook his head at the memory. "That awful night, when I saw her collapsed on the floor of the Chapter House. It was as if my prayers had been answered and I was horrified at what I'd done. It brought me to my senses. I knew I had to stop. I had spent weeks wishing her ill and she'd almost died right in front of my eyes."

"When did you start stealing money?" asked Shadow as the canon's tears continued to run down his face.

"A little over a year ago."

"Why did you do it?" asked Shadow.

"It was when the previous dean's retirement was announced. I realised in ten years or so I would be in the same position. Gwyneth and I would have to leave here – the house goes with the position of canon treasurer, you see – and I haven't been able to put much aside for our retirement. It seemed to me there wasn't going to be much to look forward to in our old age."

Hugh produced a large white handkerchief from his pocket and wiped his eyes and blew his nose loudly before walking over to his desk and unlocking the top drawer. He removed a brochure and handed it to Shadow. It was for a luxury cruise around the Mediterranean starting in Rome then calling in at Capri, Florence, Sicily and Sardinia before ending in Venice.

"The two of us have dreamt of seeing Rome again and I know Gwyneth longs to visit more of Italy. I remember seeing an advertisement in the travel agent's window for this cruise and on a whim went in and picked up a brochure. Gwyneth turns fifty next year and I thought what a perfect way to celebrate. Since her accident, travelling isn't so easy, and most of our spare money has been spent making alterations to the house, but she's never complained about how things turned out, never been angry about all things she's missed out on: a family, a career. She is so good, and I wished I could think of a way to afford to take her on this cruise. It would be a way for us to create some wonderful memories, something to look back on and enjoy as we grew older."

He paused and blew his nose again. "The first time it was a genuine mistake. A farmer was delivering some bales of straw for harvest festival and wanted to be paid in cash. I was told it would be two hundred pounds, so I withdrew the money from the bank, but he only asked for one hundred and didn't provide me with an invoice or ask for a receipt. Suddenly I found myself with a hundred pounds in my hands and I'm ashamed to say the temptation was too much. I succumbed. I issued a false receipt and brought the money home and hid it here in my desk. It was so very easy." He began to weep again as he removed a large, bulky white envelope from the desk. "At first, I tried to justify it. I told myself that Gwyneth deserved compensation for what happened to her. I purposely went in search of local suppliers who preferred to deal in cash."

"Like Ingham and Woodhouse at La Dolce Vita," interrupted Shadow, placing the invoice he had removed from Joseph's file next to the poison pen letter. Hugh looked at it and nodded.

"Yes. Then I would find a way to alter the invoice or produce a false receipt and nobody noticed, but I felt sure Clarissa would, so I tried to frighten her, make her think twice about staying here."

"How much have you taken in total?"

"Two thousand, two hundred and forty pounds," Hugh

replied immediately. He thrust the envelope towards Shadow. "Please take it, Chief Inspector, but please don't arrest me, I beg of you. I couldn't bear Gwyneth to know what I've done," he pleaded. "I couldn't bear her to think badly of me."

Shadow stood up and sighed wearily.

"I'm not going to arrest you, Mr Marchman, but you need to find a way to return that money."

The canon looked at him in amazement. "Yes, yes of course I shall. I'll think of something. I don't know how I can ever thank you, Chief Inspector."

"Start by not writing any more letters to the dean," replied Shadow. He picked up the letter and the receipt and tossed them into the flames of the roaring fire before walking out the door.

THE SNOW HAD covered the pavements in a thick white blanket that muffled his footsteps as Shadow made his way home. He considered his conversation with the canon and the risks people were prepared to take. Hugh had risked his career and good name to treat his wife to a holiday. Simon had risked his marriage for the sake of some excitement. Then there were Joe and Toby. Those two young men seemed happy to risk getting on the wrong side of the law, throwing away their education. What for? Just to make some quick cash. Neither of them had been seen in over twenty-four hours and the boat at Naburn had disappeared. Could they have been working for a criminal gang, and it had ended badly for them? Things had certainly ended badly for poor Anna Novak. It bothered him that Gwyneth Marchman was so sure she had seen Simon Fortescue on Sunday night when he was meant to have taken a sleeping tablet, but the alternative was even more unsettling.

Shadow's feet crunched down the steps of Skeldergate Bridge and *Florence* came into view, silent and dark. He couldn't help comparing it to the warm and welcoming atmosphere of the Marchmans' house. Glancing over his shoulder, he noticed the faint orange glow from the brazier next to the flimsy cardboard construction under the bridge. Jake and Missy must have exchanged Lendal for Skeldergate Bridge, following that idiot MacNab's article. *There's always someone worse off*, he thought to himself as he stepped aboard, opened the door and flicked on the light.

CHAPTER TEN

Across 8 (4 letters)
Yves found his tail in this Mediterranean country

ALTHOUGH IT WAS Saturday and the day of Jimmy and Sophie's wedding, Shadow still had some paperwork to sign off before Inspector Grabowski officially took over the investigation into Anna Novak's and David Smith's deaths. He picked up the morning suit Maggie had made him hire from where it had been hanging in its cover on the back of his bedroom door and folded it over his arm. When he stepped on to the towpath, he was surprised to see an elegant figure walking towards him along the snow-covered path. Barbara was dressed in her long black fur coat with matching hat, and Shadow didn't think for one minute her appearance was a chance meeting.

"Good morning," he said politely.

"Good morning, Chief Inspector. May I walk with you into the city?" she asked.

"Certainly."

"You live alone, I understand," she said, nodding towards *Florence*.

"Yes," replied Shadow.

She took his free arm as they climbed the steps up to Skeldergate Bridge.

"You don't even have any pets for company?"

"No."

"Neither do I anymore. Not since I moved into an apartment. When I was a child, we had both a dog and a cat. The dog, Nino, was quite naughty, always barking at our neighbours, chasing squirrels and upsetting the postman."

Shadow nodded silently as he listened to her.

"Nino was always stealing food too, if we weren't looking. The cat, Giuseppe, however, well, he too was greedy, but he did very little except sleep in the sun, coming and going as he pleased. One day, my mother had made a fish mousse, salmon I think, for a dinner party she was hosting that evening. When she had almost finished, the telephone rang, and she went into the hall to answer it. When she returned to the kitchen the mousse had disappeared. The dish, on the floor, licked clean. Naturally, Nino was blamed. She shouted at him and tied him up outside in the garden while she began the cooking again. However, as I went upstairs, I found Giuseppe stretched out on my mother's bed in a pool of sunlight, licking the remains of the mousse from his paws. He was such a greedy cat! Within an hour he was weaving himself around my mother's legs, hoping for more mousse. And do you know, she let him lick the second bowl clean, thinking he had done nothing wrong."

Barbara paused and turned to look Shadow straight in the eye.

"Isn't it strange the things we remember from our youth, Chief Inspector?"

"It is, indeed, Mrs Smith."

Shadow waited for a moment as they continued to walk together, in case she wanted to add more to her story, but it seemed she had said everything she wanted to say.

"Will you and your father be celebrating Christmas here in York?" he enquired.

"Sadly not, we have come to the conclusion that the cold, damp climate in this country is no longer suitable for Papa's health. Today we fly to South America. We have good friends there."

Shadow nodded and offered her his hand.

"Then I shall wish you a safe journey and a merry Christmas."

"Thank you, Chief Inspector."

By now they had almost reached St Helen's Square. Jimmy was arriving at the station at the same time Shadow was bidding Barbara goodbye. He was dressed in his running gear.

"What did she want, Chief?" he asked, slightly breathlessly.

"To let me know her family aren't responsible for either of the deaths we are investigating. She must have found out that we are about to put them under surveillance."

"So, who is responsible, Chief?"

"A greedy cat apparently," replied Shadow without any further elaboration as the two detectives walked into the station together.

"What are you doing here anyway? You're getting married in less than six hours."

"I was out for a run when I remembered I'd left some notes I made for my speech here, so I came to pick them up and there's a list of songs we want the DJ to play at the reception too. When everyone arrives, there's going to be a harpist playing. She'll do all classical stuff, arias from different operas – that kind of thing – then later on there'll be a disco. Hopefully, we've got something for everyone."

Shadow listened as Jimmy chattered away. He was even more talkative than usual, and Shadow wondered if it was due to nerves or excitement. Suddenly, he stopped in his tracks.

"Verdi!" he exclaimed before dumping his suit in front of a startled constable on the reception desk, turning around and striding out into St Helen's Square.

"Chief?" queried Jimmy, hurrying after him.

"It's what Barbara wanted me to know. Giuseppe the cat. In English Giuseppe is Joseph. He isn't a halfwit. I am!"

"But we couldn't find anything to link him or Toby to the murders. And they've both disappeared."

"But the cat is greedy. He returned for more and Barbara knew it," snapped Shadow, heading towards the archway that led to La Dolce Vita. Halfway down the cobbled path, there came the crashing sound of splintering wood and loud, angry shouting. Shadow and Jimmy ran down only to find the door to the shop's storeroom had been smashed in. When they looked inside, they could see three burly men, wearing balaclavas, attacking a cowering Toby and Joseph with baseball bats. Jimmy ran into the storeroom and tried pulling one of the men off Toby, only to be punched in the face himself.

"Stop! Police!" yelled Shadow. The three attackers paused, their eyes glaring at him through their masks. Then one shouted something in a language Shadow didn't understand before all three of them came charging towards him swinging their baseball bats. He managed to duck behind the door hanging off its hinges out of the way of the first two as they ran out of the storeroom, then he launched himself at the knees of the third man, bringing him crashing down to the ground. Before he had the chance to get to his feet, Shadow knelt on his back with his full weight and grabbed hold of both his wrists.

"You okay, Chief?" asked Jimmy, emerging from the storeroom, blood dripping from his nose.

"Phone for help and get after the other two," ordered Shadow, still grappling with the man on the floor. He was struggling so much that it felt like he was on a bucking bronco. After what felt like an eternity, but was probably no more than a few minutes, several uniformed officers came slipping and sliding down the snowy path.

"Give me some cuffs," shouted Shadow. Miraculously, in one fluid movement, he managed to catch the cuffs the first constable threw to him and clasped them around the wrists of the man who continued to shout, swear and kick his legs.

"Oh, calm down," said Shadow, quite exhausted from the struggle.

Jimmy reappeared, also out of breath. "They drove off, but I got their number and I've put a call out," he panted as Tom and several more uniformed officers came running down the cobbled path.

"What's going on, Chief?" asked the constable, offering Shadow his hand. From his uncomfortable position on the man's back, Shadow staggered to his feet and motioned to the still flailing and shouting thug.

"Get him on his feet and tell the custody sergeant he's about to have a guest. Then call an ambulance for those two, Tom," said Shadow, pointing to Joe and Toby, who were both still groaning in agony inside the storeroom. "You had better get looked over too," he said to Jimmy, whose left eye was now purply red and getting more swollen by the second.

"Sophie's going to kill me," his sergeant groaned as he tried to look at his reflection in the broken glass around the storeroom door.

"She'll have to wait. Make yourself useful. Find out who he is and read him his rights," ordered Shadow, gesturing to the man who, now upright, was struggling and swearing at

Tom and another constable. Jimmy approached him, removed his balaclava and gasped.

"Oh my God, Chief. It's the Snowman! The guy Inspector Grabowski has been after for ages."

"Really? Well then I suppose it was worth a black eye," replied Shadow. He turned to Tom. "Send his photo and fingerprints to the Albanian police. Let's see if we can finally find out his real name."

The man under arrest swore and spat on the ground.

"Charming," replied Shadow. He ducked into the storeroom and beckoned to two uniformed officers to follow him. The door to the tunnel was wide open. Shadow peered down. There was a large cruiser, its deck loaded with boxes tied up at the end. It was clear Joe and Toby were trying to remove the remaining stock from the shop without being seen.

"Joseph Ingham, I am arresting you on suspicion of causing the deaths of David Smith and Anna Novak," began Shadow as one of the constables placed handcuffs on the young man.

"What's going on, Joe?" interrupted Toby in bewilderment, blood pouring from his mouth as he nursed a badly bruised hand. "Who the hell were those guys?"

"They were Albanian gangsters, upset about you and Mr Ingham cutting the cocaine you bought from them, or rather didn't buy from them, as Joe stole the money back after he killed Mr Smith. Not only did you steal from them, but you were in danger of drawing far too much attention to yourselves and by extension to their activities too. I'm sure Mr Smith would have warned you about the men you wanted to do business with. You should have listened to him."

"The accountant guy?" asked Toby, looking even more confused than ever.

"He wasn't an accountant. He was a go-between. The connection between you and a particularly nasty and violent group of gentlemen based in Leeds," explained Shadow.

"Oh my God, Joe! I thought we were just trying to pass off cheap plonk as vintage wine. You said it would be a doddle!"

"Don't be so dense, Toby! Drugs is where the real money is, not booze," snapped Joseph. "Honestly, you're so thick! I've always had to carry you! If you weren't so slow, we could have been out of here before those thugs found us."

"I imagine they were quite upset about you killing someone who worked for them. If I were you, Joe, I would think very carefully about your options. You might find it's actually much safer to be in prison," said Shadow as the two ambulances, their sirens blaring, rattled down the cobbled path.

WHEN THEY ARRIVED at the hospital, it became clear that Toby was every bit as clueless as he had always appeared.

Despite Shadow explaining the situation to him twice, he still couldn't grasp that he could be charged with fraud, supplying class A drugs and being an accessory to murder.

"We were only selling wine on the cheap," he kept repeating. "My dad's going to kill me."

"It really isn't him you should be worried about," murmured Shadow as he left while a nurse bandaged his hand.

Joseph, however, was guarded and defensive. The meek and mild person they had first encountered had completely disappeared.

"You can't prove I was responsible for Smith's death," he said as soon as Shadow walked into the room where he was waiting to be taken for an X-ray. "You might be able to get me on fraud or false accounting, but you would have arrested me earlier if you'd had enough evidence."

"You are quite correct," replied Shadow calmly. "We were struggling to find a link, but I'm sure the Albanian gentleman we have in custody will be able to explain why you were meeting Mr Smith in the hotel and why you needed to stop him reporting back to the people who had sent him to speak to you. He's facing an extremely long sentence and will be keen to help us, especially if it means getting his revenge on a young man who double-crossed him."

Joe stared at him, and Shadow could almost see the young man's brain working out his best course of action, as if it was a complicated equation.

"It was an accident," he declared finally.

"An accident? You hit him over the head with one of the stone ornaments in the hotel room, then no doubt remembering the story of how one of Barbara's husbands died, tried to make it look like he'd slipped and fallen. Unfortunately, you hadn't accounted for Anna, noticing the bottle of wine. Greco Salice Salentino really was your downfall. Without it, you would never have come to our attention."

"He was threatening me. I had to defend myself," insisted Joe.

Shadow stood up. "That is something to discuss with your legal team," he said, turning to go.

"I'm willing to cooperate. I'll tell you everything I know about him and his gang if you put me into witness protection."

There was now a note of panic in the young man's voice.

"As I said, speak with your solicitor, Mr Ingham," repeated Shadow, thinking what a waste it was that such an intelligent young man couldn't have put his brains to better use.

"Anna was nothing to do with me," Joe shouted after him. Shadow glanced back at him. "I'll admit to hitting Smith, but I never laid a finger on Anna. I never saw her after she finished cleaning the shop on Friday." There was something in the young man's expression that made Shadow wonder if he could be telling the truth.

AFTER ENSURING THERE were uniformed officers guarding Joe and Toby while they were treated for cracked ribs and a collection of broken fingers and noses, Shadow went in search of Jimmy. He found him sitting on a trolley behind a curtain in A&E staring woefully at his face in a small, plastic hand mirror.

"Chief. I can't look like this in my wedding photos," he groaned.

"You'll have to have them taken in profile," agreed Shadow, wincing at Jimmy's left eye, that was now so swollen it was completely closed.

"Sophie's going to kill me," he repeated.

"She'll just be pleased you aren't seriously injured," Shadow reassured him.

"And Tom's been in touch. The two guys who got away crashed their car heading back to Leeds and have been arrested."

"Good, was anyone injured?"

"No, but the A64 is closed now while they investigate the crash. I bet half our guests won't be able to get to York."

Shadow thought this may well be true but tried to think of something positive to cheer up his beleaguered sergeant.

"On the plus side, you did get to arrest West Yorkshire's most wanted man. All that reading about gangsters paid off finally."

Jimmy attempted a weak smile. "That's true. Inspector Grabowski has already phoned to congratulate me, and Tom said the chief constable's secretary called to say they are putting my name forward for a commendation. By the way, Inspector Grabowski is coming over to collect the Snowman, Chief."

"Let's start calling him by his real name, Sergeant. He's Ilir Bardhi. Apparently, the Albanian police have confirmed his identity from the fingerprints we took. He's wanted there too."

"Okay, but why did he and the other two guys attack Tom and Joe?"

"Because they, or at least Joe, had stolen drugs from them. I think Joe has always been desperate to be rich; perhaps it stemmed from being the scholarship boy at a school full of much wealthier children, like Toby. However, rather than use his brains to forge a legitimate career, he thought he could outsmart criminals, but he needed Toby and his money to get him started.

"He took the cocaine from Smith but didn't pay for it. You see, the strength of the Albanians' organisation was also their weakness. Because they didn't rely on mobiles or modern technology, there was a time lag. Smith came to La Dolce Vita telling Toby he was an accountant, but really it was to supply Joe with cocaine from the Albanians. Joe planned to use his cover of giving free drinks away to start supplying drugs. He showed Smith the money in the safe, the money for the rent, but told him he couldn't give it to him until that evening so Toby wouldn't notice. Smith agreed and booked into the hotel. He made two very short phone calls to let Joe and Bardhi know where he was. That evening Joe entered the hotel via the fire escape with the cash and the bottle of wine."

"As a gesture of goodwill?" asked Jimmy.

"Partly, but mainly I think he was using it as part of his disguise. I think he dressed in black shirt and trousers like the rest of the staff. If anyone saw him carrying a bottle of wine, they would simply think he was one of the waiters. Unfortunately, he'd chosen Greco Salice Salentino. Any other bottle and we might never have linked him to Smith's death."

"Yes, it was only after Sophie mentioned it was the same wine the dean had drunk that you asked her to look at Smith's post-mortem notes again," agreed Jimmy.

Shadow nodded. "I think Smith opened the wine as he was counting the money. While he was distracted, Joe hit him over the head and then moved his body to the bathroom, making it look like an accident, an idea he got after speaking to Don Rossetti, who told him the story of how one of Barbara's husbands died. However, he didn't bargain for Anna finding the body. She was a bright girl who no doubt recognised the wine as coming from La Dolce Vita and recalled the story that Don Rossetti had probably shared with her too. She wasn't sure who was to blame for Smith's death, but having worked out who Don Rossetti really was, a gangster, not just a lonely old man, she was scared.

"Meanwhile Bardhi didn't receive a call from Smith telling him he had the money, so he arrived at the hotel only to hear staff discussing how a guest had died supposedly after an accident. He left the city, but Joe started drawing attention to himself by being greedy and cutting the cocaine with boric acid, making his customers ill. Barbara and others soon realised what was going on. Incidentally he returned the cash to the safe, but forgot to change the combination so Toby couldn't pay Barbara on Friday morning."

"Why didn't Barbara tell you all this? Why come up with some story about a cat?"

"She knew we were watching her and her father. She wanted to protect him, as he had tried so hard to protect her, by letting me know who we should be focusing our attention on. However, she wasn't about to say something that might risk her being called back to give evidence and draw attention to herself and her father. Instead, she told me an innocent tale from her childhood and hoped I would understand."

"Wow, that's one clever woman! What about Anna?"

Shadow shook his head and frowned.

"It would make sense for Joe to have killed her to keep her quiet, but he swears he didn't, and he has an alibi for Sunday night. There's something else that's bothering me too," he added, almost to himself.

"Chief?" queried Jimmy, but Shadow patted him on the back.

"Enough of the case, it's Grabowski's problem now. I need to get back to the station and you need to get yourself cleaned up. The clock's ticking."

"Tell me about it," said Jimmy. "Can you do me a favour, Chief? Let Sophie know what's been going on. I don't want her to be shocked when she sees me as she walks down the aisle. I was going to call, but they don't like you to use your phone here and then I thought it might be unlucky."

Shadow despaired at his sergeant still bothering about superstitions, but all he said was: "Yes, of course. Leave it to me. I'll see you at the Minster."

SHADOW RETURNED TO the station and signed the necessary forms for handing Bardhi over to Inspector Grabowski, who was on her way over from Leeds, but had been delayed by the getaway car crashing. Then he retrieved his morning suit from reception and quickly changed in his office, before hurrying down snow-covered Stonegate to the Minster. George was on duty at the door, making sure only wedding guests entered.

"What a day!" he exclaimed. "I thought I'd be the only one running late, but even the groom isn't here yet?"

"What happened to you?" asked Shadow.

"I was on duty here. I thought I'd have a nice quiet morning before going to collect Carol in time for the wedding. Then Canon Marchman came around to the office in a real flap. It seemed some money had been found at the office that morning. An anonymous charitable donation was posted through the door and needed to be paid into the bank immediately. It was over two thousand pounds, so he wanted me to go with him. I went to meet him at the office and, unfortunately, Marjorie was there too. You can imagine, she wanted all the paperwork for receiving the donation to be signed in triplicate." Shadow nodded sympathetically as George carried on. "Then when I got back from the bank it was time to go and get Carol. The traffic was terrible. The Leeds road is blocked, so everyone was taking a detour through the city. Where's the groom? Is he on his way?"

"He should be here any minute," replied Shadow as he entered the Minster. "Where's the bride?"

SHADOW FOUND SOPHIE in the vestry. She was pacing up and down in her beautiful white lace gown, her blonde hair piled up and secured by a sparkling tiara with a long veil hanging down her back. Her face turned pale when she saw Shadow standing in the doorway.

"Oh my God! What's happened? I knew it must be something bad. Jimmy would never be late unless something had happened to him."

"He's fine, Sophie. He's fine," insisted Shadow, stepping forward and hoping he sounded reassuring. "He called in to the station after his run and got caught up in an incident at the wine shop we've been investigating. He would have called, but he couldn't use his mobile at the hospital." Sophie's hand flew to her mouth. "But he's fine," continued Shadow quickly. Then he paused and cleared his throat. "But he has got a black eye. He asked me to say sorry if he looks a mess. He didn't want it to be a shock when you walked down the aisle and he thought it would be bad luck if he tried to see you before the ceremony."

Sophie's face broke into a smile as she exhaled with relief. "I couldn't care less how he looks, as long as he's okay. As for bad luck – half the guests are delayed. The guy who was meant to be filming the ceremony has texted to say he's held up on the A64 and won't be able to get here. Now the groom is injured. Honestly, what else can go wrong?"

"I can take the video, if you want?" offered Tom, who had now arrived in the vestry. He was following behind Angela, carrying the train of her burgundy velvet bridesmaid dress. "I've got my camera with me. I was going to do a bit of informal filming at the reception."

"Sophie's just said she doesn't want anything else to go wrong," snapped Shadow, who still hadn't quite forgiven the young constable for the mix-up over Anna Novak's nationality.

"He's quite good, you know," said Angela. "Show him the video you took at the quiz night, Tom, while I redo Sophie's make-up. I know you're nervous, Soph, but stop licking your lips. You've taken all the gloss off," she continued, chiding the bride as she also shooed the two policemen out of the vestry. Tom began rummaging through a large camera bag he was carrying on his shoulder before producing a laptop that he duly flicked open.

"It was a great night, Chief. I've already edited and uploaded it. Don't worry, you won't have to watch the whole quiz. I'll start it when the trophy was awarded," he said as an image of a packed Lendal Cellars appeared on the screen.

"Do you often carry all this paraphernalia around with you?" asked Shadow as he placed his glasses on the end of his nose and peered at the image.

"It's a bit of a hobby of mine. I was planning on doing some informal filming at the reception, Chief. After the professional guy had finished. You know, getting everyone to record a message for the bride and groom. Something they can look back on. You never get chance to talk to everyone properly at a wedding."

Shadow wasn't listening; he was concentrating on the film of the quiz night. Ben and Ollie were holding the trophy aloft amidst much cheering. Then the film had been edited to later in the evening, when after quite a few drinks had obviously been downed, Ben was leading the revellers in a conga out of Lendal Cellars and into the cobbled street.

"It did get a bit raucous. We ended up singing carols around the Christmas tree in St Helen's Square," explained Tom apologetically. "But I'm quite pleased with how I handled moving from the bright lights of the pub into the darkness outside and I didn't lose focus…"

Shadow held up his hand to silence him.

"Rewind that bit," ordered Shadow. Tom obediently did as he was told.

There it was walking in the opposite direction to the oblivious revellers, a dark figure wearing a hat, their face obscured, heading towards La Dolce Vita.

"Well, what's the verdict, Chief? Did I do a good enough job to film the ceremony? What do you think?" the young man asked eagerly.

"Tom," said Shadow, trying to keep the irritation out of his voice. "Did it never occur to you that it might have been helpful to show me a video you took on the night one of our murder victims died before now?"

The young man's face fell. "I'm sorry, Chief. I didn't think," he stammered.

"Never mind, I think you might have finally redeemed yourself. Make sure you don't delete that video," replied Shadow, patting the young man on the back as he strode towards the quire. It seemed Joe Ingham was right to protest his innocence when it came to Anna's death.

His footsteps echoed around the Minster as he hurried towards the quire. He stepped around one of the huge stone pillars and almost crashed into Canon and Mrs Marchman. Hugh's usually solemn face broke into a huge smile when he saw Shadow.

"Ah there you are, Chief Inspector," he said, grasping Shadow firmly by the hand. "I'm so pleased I found you. I wanted to thank you for the…" he paused and glanced down at his wife "…the advice you gave me last night."

"Not at all," replied Shadow, "and congratulations. I understand the Minster received an anonymous donation this morning. You must be very pleased."

"Yes indeed," said Hugh, the colour rising to his cheeks.

"That's not the only cause for celebration. Tell him, Hugh," said Gwyneth, giving her husband a little nudge.

"A most fortuitous turn of events. One might almost say a miracle," Hugh began to explain, his smile growing even wider. "A little over an hour ago, I received a telephone call from His Grace, the archbishop. It seems our ambassador to the Holy See has requested early retirement and the archbishop, after consulting the previous dean, was kind enough to put my name forward. We leave in the New Year."

"The archbishop said he could think of nobody better," chimed in Gwyneth, her voice full of pride. "We shall miss York, of course. We have been very happy here, but you know how we have longed to see Italy again, Chief Inspector. Just think, in a few weeks' time, we shall actually be living in Rome."

"I'm very happy for you both," replied Shadow.

"Thank you, Chief Inspector. Now if you will excuse me, I must go and tell the dean. I would hate for her to hear our news from anyone else."

Shadow watched Hugh hurry away. He looked like a totally different person from the man he'd left sobbing in his study the previous evening. He felt a light touch on his arm and turned to see Gwyneth smiling up at him.

"I don't know what you said to him last night, Chief Inspector, and I don't want to know, but I would like to add my thanks. He remained alone in his study for quite some time after you'd left, but when he came out, it was as if a huge burden had been lifted from his shoulders. Something had been bothering him, weighing him down for months, something he clearly felt he couldn't share with me. I was becoming quite worried, but it's gone now and suddenly we have so much to look forward to. As Hugh said, it is almost miraculous how our lives will change."

"Perhaps it's true when they say the Lord works in mysterious ways," suggested Shadow, relieved that she wasn't expecting him to share his conversation with her husband. Gwyneth gave him a sidelong glance.

"Do you know something, Chief Inspector? I've never liked that hymn very much. I've always found his instructions to be quite easy to follow. Be kind, see the best in others, treat them as you would wish to be treated and always be willing to ask for and to dispense forgiveness. It really is very simple, not mysterious at all. Now if you'll excuse me,

I've promised to assist the organist. His regular page turner is stuck in traffic apparently."

She turned and wheeled herself up the ramp to where the huge organ was housed. Shadow followed her through the doors and into the quire, where the guests were shuffling in their seats and murmuring about the delay to proceedings, as Ben and Ollie tried to reassure them. Despite the problems with the snow and traffic, the place was still packed with Jimmy's and Sophie's nearest and dearest. Shadow waved and nodded to an anxious-looking Rose and Jimmy's grandfather.

Maggie had saved him a seat next to her. She was wearing a silk dress in her favourite emerald green and a huge matching hat.

"You look very nice," he said, sliding into the pew.

"Thank you. What's going on? I was starting to think you weren't coming."

"I wouldn't miss Jimmy and Sophie's wedding," bristled Shadow.

"No need to sound so offended. A couple of years ago, we would never have seen you at a wedding no matter who was getting married, but you've been much better recently," she conceded.

"Maybe that's thanks to you," ventured Shadow.

Maggie blushed a little and gave her head a shake. "Actually, I would give Jimmy most of the credit. He's managed to wear down that grumpy veneer of yours. The two of you make quite a team. He certainly looks up to you. Maybe he sees you as a sort of father figure."

Shadow raised a sceptical eyebrow. "I hardly think so!"

"All right that might be a bit of a stretch," agreed Maggie. "Not a father, an uncle then – and not a favourite uncle, of course, not the fun sort, but the type you'd go to for advice on getting a mortgage or something."

Shadow grinned despite himself. "That sounds more like it."

He glanced over to where Simon and Clarissa Fortescue were standing together consulting their watches. Suddenly, Jimmy came hurrying down the aisle, nodding apologetically while still tying his cravat, before taking his place in front the dean next to Ben and Ollie. A second later the organ struck up and all heads turned as Sophie glided elegantly down the aisle on the arm of her father, who was beaming proudly.

Apart from a brief moment of confusion between Ben and Ollie as to which of them had the rings, the ceremony went smoothly, and Shadow watched along with the other guests as Clarissa declared they were now man and wife. He handed Maggie his handkerchief when he noticed her brushing a tear away as the harpist began to play.

"What a beautiful ceremony," she said wistfully as Jimmy and Sophie were joined by the bridal party to sign the register. "Didn't you think so?"

"Very nice," agreed Shadow, although in truth, his mind had been mostly occupied with when he could act on what he'd seen in Tom's video, bearing in mind Sophie's wish that nothing else should spoil the day. She might be one of the most serene brides he'd ever seen but having her new husband's boss disappear to arrest a murderer during her reception might be too much even for her.

The reception was to be held in a large white marquee that had been erected in Dean's Park. Maggie took Shadow's arm as they left the Minster and walked along the narrow pathway that had been cleared through the snow and covered in a red carpet. Christmas trees festooned with fairy lights stood on either side of the entrance and inside it was decorated with white candles and wreaths and garlands of holly and mistletoe. The guests were served canapés and champagne while classical music played softly in the background. The happy couple were posing for photographs. Shadow smiled to himself as both Tom and the official photographer tried to find an angle where Jimmy's swollen eye was less noticeable. He turned to see Maggie watching him intently.

"You look almost jovial. Is it the happy couple or have you finally found your Christmas spirit?" she asked.

"Maybe both, but it is nice to see Jimmy and Sophie so happy."

"Bless him, Jimmy can't wait to go skiing. He was telling me all about it earlier," she said, sitting down next to him.

Shadow grunted. "It's a good thing he's married a doctor. I'm expecting him to return with most of his limbs in a plaster cast."

"I think it sounds very romantic. An alpine lodge at Christmas with roaring log fires and snow falling outside. Cuddled up together, opening presents by the tree and drinking mulled wine."

Shadow groaned. "There'll be even more of that stuff over there than there is here. And I think the freezing snow will lose its appeal when they have both got chapped lips and chilblains. I'd prefer a bit of winter sun any day."

"Is that so? Then it seems like the perfect time to give you this."

Maggie slipped an envelope with a red satin bow tied around it across the table to him.

"What is it?

"Your present from me. Merry Christmas."

"It's a bit early, isn't it?"

"The usual response is 'thank you', John."

Shadow carefully removed the ribbon and opened the envelope. Inside was a plane ticket to Brindisi.

"I thought we might be spending Christmas together," he said gruffly.

Maggie gave his hand a quick squeeze. "Perhaps next year," she replied softly. "I think it's time you went out there and said goodbye, don't you?"

Shadow nodded and leaning across the table, gently kissed her cheek.

"Thank you, Maggie," he said quietly. Then before he could say any more the tapping of a fork against a champagne glass told the guests that the speeches were about to start. Sophie's father was up first. He looked as if he hated public speaking every bit as much as Shadow and managed to say everything that was expected of him in under two minutes.

Then it was Jimmy's turn. He reduced half the guests to tears as he told them all how much he loved Sophie and how happy she made him. Up next were Ben and Ollie, who had the audience in stitches with their stories about working with Sophie and Jimmy. Shadow couldn't help but notice that most of the jokes seemed to be at his expense.

After the speeches, the disco started, and everyone seemed to relax. Shadow went to offer his congratulations to the groom.

"Will you cope without me, Chief?" asked Jimmy, who hadn't stopped grinning all day.

"I won't need to. I'm going to spend Christmas with Luca and his family."

Jimmy's eyes opened in surprise. "But you never leave Yorkshire, let alone the country."

"The decision wasn't entirely my own."

Jimmy's smile faded a little. "You are coming back, aren't you, Chief?"

"What do you mean?"

"Well, you love everything about Italy – the food, the wine – and you and Luca got on really well. Maybe when you are out there in the sun, you won't want to come back."

Shadow shook his head. "If that is the case, then I'm sure you'll cope without me, Sergeant."

DUE TO THE problems with traffic and the ever-increasing snow, Jimmy and Sophie decided to depart earlier than planned and leave their guests to enjoy the evening disco. In a nod to Sophie's horse-riding childhood, a carriage and four horses was to take them as far as the station where a taxi would be waiting for them.

There was quite a crowd gathered in front of the Minster to watch the happy couple leave. Shadow spotted a few familiar faces. There was Dorothy the director of the Eboracum Museum with her partner Genevieve, Matthew and Celia, two of the ghost walk guides, Oliver from Bacchus and even Malcolm Webster, who was being scolded by Marjorie for throwing confetti.

As the rest of the wedding party were waving off the happy couple, Shadow realised he could put off his duty no longer. He went and spoke quietly to George. Then he turned and surveyed the crowd. Maggie was comforting a weeping Rose. Angela was celebrating catching Sophie's bouquet, while Ben and Ollie teased a blushing Tom. Simon Fortescue was entertaining the Marchmans with some tale about his own wedding. Clarissa was shaking hands and saying goodbye to Sophie's parents, who were looking almost as emotional as Rose.

With a heavy heart, Shadow made his way over, hoping he wasn't about to ruin the day for everyone.

"I think you should come with me," he said softly.

The dean turned her head slightly and jutted out her chin. "Why is that, Chief Inspector?" she asked.

"Because Sergeant Hedley is waiting to arrest you for the murder of Anna Novak," he whispered.

"I see. Well, as we are on Minster land, I suppose this is his jurisdiction," she replied with a forced smile. To anyone watching to would seem like they were simply discussing the wedding. Luckily Sophie's parents were now well out of earshot.

"How did you find out?" she asked.

"I began to wonder if you could have been involved when I visited you the other night. You knew Anna's name, although it hadn't been given in the press reports. You certainly had a motive. Then I realised that you weren't Simon's alibi, he was yours. You saw a message from Anna on his phone when he left it in the vestry. You smashed screen so he would never see it."

"Simon had never been very discreet. He would quite frequently leave his phone lying around and I often read his messages. Mostly they amused me, and I knew Simon needed a distraction, needed to be entertained while I was busy working, but Anna wasn't like the others, she needed him, and he was beginning to fall in love with her. They had discussed running away together. The text I read from her said how she was looking forward to Monday and what a relief if would be. A chill went through me; I thought Simon was going to leave me the next day. Then Anna sent another text, the one he didn't read, saying she wanted to see him after she finished work and if he could get away. She said she'd be waiting at in the basement of the wine shop all night if necessary."

Shadow nodded. Until now he had only been able to guess what might have been in Anna's message, but it was what he had assumed.

"Anna was looking forward to Monday because she was planning to meet me and tell me about a crime she had witnessed. To discuss it with a police officer would be a relief," he explained. Clarissa blinked at him several times, then shook her head.

"It makes no difference. She still wanted to take him away from me. He would have gone to her if I hadn't been taken ill."

"Then when you returned from the hospital, you encouraged him to take a sleeping pill, waited a little while, then dressed up in his hat and coat, playing the male like you did at school. It was you who told me about that, but your real mistake was that ridiculous charade of smashing the glass in your office to try to distract me. If you had lived in York a little longer, perhaps you would have known that the city walls are locked at dusk. Nobody could have thrown that stone except you, before dashing inside in time for us to arrive. You were frightened Simon might say something incriminating."

"Why didn't you arrest me last night?"

"I didn't have any proof. It was only when I happened to see a video of you caught in the background quite by chance. You were heading towards La Dolce Vita. The person I saw was dressed in Simon's hat and coat, but they were limping."

"Anna could only see my silhouette through the top of the glass door, so she let me in without thinking," Clarissa continued, as if lost in the memory.

"And you hit her over the head with a cobble you picked up from outside."

"That wasn't my intention, Chief Inspector. At first, I only wanted to speak to her. Tell her to leave Simon alone. Then I saw her through the window. Waiting there, so young and beautiful. Waiting for my husband. Some primal emotion overtook me."

"Envy, wrath, perhaps even pride," suggested Shadow. The dean didn't appear to be listening, as she continued to speak.

"Having an allergic reaction to that wine was a godsend, Chief Inspector. As I was lying in hospital, I suddenly realised what I needed to do. It was like a revelation. I should go and see her instead. Explain to her that I wouldn't allow Simon to leave me. He needs me, you see. That's what none of these young girls ever understand. Simon needs me."

Shadow had heard enough. He took her firmly by the elbow and guided her to where a grim-faced George was waiting. He could hear Simon call out after them.

"Clarissa, darling, where are you going?"

She didn't look at him, instead she turned to Shadow.

"Wouldn't you do anything you could to stop the one you loved from leaving you?"

Shadow stared into the eyes of the woman standing opposite him, but all he could see was the image of Anna's soaking, lifeless body on the stretcher.

"Almost anything," he replied, then stepped back and let George read the dean her rights.

IT DIDN'T TAKE him long to pack. He glanced around the boat that had been his home for almost thirty years. He added Luisa's photo to the top of his pile of clothes in the suitcase. There was nothing else he needed. In truth, there was little else on board *Florence* to show that he had lived there for over half his life. The bookcase was full of books that he had no intention of reading again. Despite his initial protests, Jimmy had added his vast collection of jazz albums to his phone. Was it uploading or downloading? He could never remember. There was, however, one more thing he had to do before leaving for the airport.

He stepped out on to the snow-covered deck and peered

through the darkness to the orange glow beneath Skeldergate Bridge, which seemed to have become Jake's home since he abandoned the area where they found Anna.

"We've made an arrest," he called out, his warm breath forming clouds in the freezing air as he approached the young man and his dog huddled together in a sleeping bag. Jake took a drag on his cigarette.

"Good. Will they go down for it?"

"Yes, they've confessed. Are you looking for somewhere to stay over Christmas?"

Jake looked up at him, narrowing his eyes and not bothering to remove the cigarette from his mouth.

"Is that an invitation?"

"Sort of," replied Shadow with a shrug. "I'm going away for a few weeks. I need someone to keep an eye on *Florence*."

After surveying him for a moment more, Jake rose to his feet and picked up his rucksack and sleeping bag. Slightly warily, he followed Shadow back down the towpath and stepped on to the boat, with Missy leaping after him. Shadow dropped the keys to *Florence* into his hand.

"There isn't much in the fridge, but you'd better eat that lot before it goes off," he said, gesturing through the door to the hamper of Italian food Maria and Gino had given him for Christmas. Jake turned and looked at him.

"You are coming back, aren't you, Shadow?"

"That's the second time someone's asked me that."

"And?"

"You just keep Missy off the sofas and no smoking inside," replied Shadow as he hauled his suitcase on to the towpath and set off towards the bridge. "And don't upset the geese," he added as an afterthought.

A cool breeze blew across the river and a few flakes of snow began to swirl down from the sky. He glanced back. Jake had gone inside, but Missy was still sitting on the boat's prow wagging her tail.

"Merry Christmas, Missy," he called out and smiled to himself before disappearing into the darkness of the bridge's shadow.

The End

Want more? Check out John Shadow's latest case in
A Forgotten Shadow!

Join Tule Publishing's newsletter for more great reads and weekly deals!

Author's Note

A Christmas Shadow is a work of fiction, but it does include a couple of real events that I used for inspiration. The Advent Procession, at the beginning of the story, takes place as I described each year and is well worth experiencing if you have the chance. Like Shadow, I too remember seeing the Minster on fire when it was struck by lightning in 1984 and it is something I always think about whenever there is a thunderstorm in York.

All the characters in the story are imaginary except for Gerald and Donald, the two Minster cats. Sadly, Gerald really has passed away, but his statue stands in the grounds of Holy Trinity Church, Goodramgate.

ACKNOWLEDGEMENTS

Many thanks as always to the wonderful team at Tule: Jane Porter, Meghan Farrell, Cyndi Parent and Nikki Babri.

Once again, I have been incredibly lucky to work with three amazing editors: Sinclair Sawhney, Helena Newton and Beth Attwood. Thank you for all your advice, support and patience!

Huge thanks also to Patrick Knowles for another beautiful book cover and to Lee Hyat for coordinating the design.

A Christmas Shadow Crossword

1.								2.			
3.				4.							
								5.		6.	
						7.					
					8.					
			9.								

Across

2. Wilma replaces Vera to produce something new from the vine

3. Mr E's Tin was used to make this cathedral

5. Ned joins a priest under a bishop

8. Yves found his tail in this Mediterranean country

9. Keep your pet and rice as proof of purchase

Down

1. Initially Zoe and Zelda meld with Bee to obtain funds fraudulently

2. We celebrate our union with dinner, dancing and gin

4. Treat hen kindly; don't scare her

6. If you yell with George, Ann and Rob, you'll have a nasty reaction

7. An ace coin is needed to buy an illicit drug

A CHRISTMAS SHADOW CROSSWORD SOLUTION

1. E								2. W	I	N	E
3. M	I	N	S	4. T	E	R		E			
B				H				D			
E				R				5. D	E	6. A	N
Z				E				I		L	
Z				A		7. C		N		L	
L				T		O		G		E	
E				E		C				R	
D				N		A				G	
						8. I	T	A	L	Y	
						N					
			9. R	E	C	E	I	P	T		

249

If you enjoyed *A Christmas Shadow*, you'll love the other books in…

THE CHIEF INSPECTOR SHADOW SERIES

Book 1: *A Long Shadow*

Book 2: *A Viking's Shadow*

Book 3: *A Ghostly Shadow*

Book 4: *A Roman Shadow*

Book 5: *A Forgotten Shadow*

Book 6: *A Christmas Shadow*

Available now at your favorite online retailer!

ABOUT THE AUTHOR

H L Marsay always loved detective stories and promised herself that one day, she would write one too. She is lucky enough to live in York, a city full of history and mystery. When not writing, the five men in her life keep her busy – two sons, two dogs and one husband.

Thank you for reading

A Christmas Shadow

If you enjoyed this book, you can find more from all our great authors at TulePublishing.com, or from your favorite online retailer.

TULE
PUBLISHING

Printed in Great Britain
by Amazon

10271218R00150